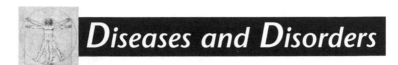
Diseases and Disorders

Deafness

by Barbara Sheen

LUCENT BOOKS
An imprint of Thomson Gale, a part of The Thomson Corporation

THOMSON
GALE

Detroit • New York • San Francisco • San Diego • New Haven, Conn.
Waterville, Maine • London • Munich

LIBRARY OF CONGRESS CATALOGING-IN-PUBLICATION DATA

Sheen, Barbara.
  Deafness / by Barbara Sheen.
    p. cm. — (Diseases and disorders)
  Includes bibliographical references and index.
  Contents: What is deafness?—Diagnosis and treatment—Many ways to communicate—Living with deafness—What the future holds.
    ISBN 1-59018-408-4 (hard cover : alk. paper)
    1. Deafness. I. Title. II. Series: Diseases and disorders series
    RF290.S49 2005
    617.8—dc22
                                                                    2005011530

Printed in the United States of America

Table of Contents

Foreword   4

Introduction
  Lack of Knowledge Leads to Problems   6

Chapter 1
  What Is Deafness?   11

Chapter 2
  Diagnosis and Treatment   27

Chapter 3
  Many Ways to Communicate   43

Chapter 4
  Living with Deafness   59

Chapter 5
  What the Future Holds   75

  Notes   91
  Glossary   95
  Organizations to Contact   98
  For Further Reading   101
  Works Consulted   103
  Index   107
  Picture Credits   111
  About the Author   112

"The Most Difficult Puzzles Ever Devised"

C HARLES BEST, ONE of the pioneers in the search for a cure for diabetes, once explained what it is about medical research that intrigued him so. "It's not just the gratification of knowing one is helping people," he confided, "although that probably is a more heroic and selfless motivation. Those feelings may enter in, but truly, what I find best is the feeling of going toe to toe with nature, of trying to solve the most difficult puzzles ever devised. The answers are there somewhere, those keys that will solve the puzzle and make the patient well. But how will those keys be found?"

Since the dawn of civilization, nothing has so puzzled people—and often frightened them, as well—as the onset of illness in a body or mind that had seemed healthy before. A seizure, the inability of a heart to pump, the sudden deterioration of muscle tone in a small child—being unable to reverse such conditions or even to understand why they occur was unspeakably frustrating to healers. Even before there were names for such conditions, even before they were understood at all, each was a reminder of how complex the human body was, and how vulnerable.

While our grappling with understanding diseases has been frustrating at times, it has also provided some of humankind's most heroic accomplishments. Alexander Fleming's accidental discovery in 1928 of a mold that could be turned into penicillin has resulted in the saving of untold millions of lives. The isolation of the enzyme insulin has reversed what was once a death sentence for anyone with diabetes. There have been great strides in combating conditions for which there is not yet a cure, too. Medicines can help AIDS patients live longer, diagnostic tools such as mammography and ultrasounds can help doctors find tumors while they are treatable, and laser surgery techniques have made the most intricate, minute operations routine.

This "toe-to-toe" competition with diseases and disorders is even more remarkable when seen in a historical continuum. An astonishing amount of progress has been made in a very short time. Just two hundred years ago, the existence of germs as a cause of some diseases was unknown. In fact, it was less than 150 years ago that a British surgeon named Joseph Lister had difficulty persuading his fellow doctors that washing their hands before delivering a baby might increase the chances of a healthy delivery (especially if they had just attended to a diseased patient)!

Each book in Lucent's Diseases and Disorders series explores a disease or disorder and the knowledge that has been accumulated (or discarded) by doctors through the years. Each book also examines the tools used for pinpointing a diagnosis, as well as the various means that are used to treat or cure a disease. Finally, new ideas are presented—techniques or medicines that may be on the horizon.

Frustration and disappointment are still part of medicine, for not every disease or condition can be cured or prevented. But the limitations of knowledge are being pushed outward constantly; the "most difficult puzzles ever devised" are finding challengers every day.

Lack of Knowledge Leads to Problems

ELIZABETH, JESSICA, JONATHAN, and Sean are all high school students. Like all teenagers, they have a variety of interests. Elizabeth is a varsity athlete. Jonathan is an honor-roll student. Sean and Jessica are writers. All are typical teenagers, except for one difference—they are deaf.

These young people are not alone. One out of every ten Americans has some degree of hearing loss. Some of these individuals have only minor hearing problems, but one out of every four hundred, or approximately 2 million Americans, are profoundly deaf, unable to hear normal speech or everyday sounds.

Since deafness has no visible symptoms, it is almost impossible to distinguish hearing-impaired people from others. The condition affects males and females of every age, ethnicity, and social background.

Ignorance Leads to Misconceptions

Because deafness cannot be seen, many hearing people have never knowingly come in contact with deaf people. Moreover, since deafness is not life threatening, it receives little coverage by the media. As a result, most people do not know much about hearing loss or the issues that deaf people face. Ignorance about deafness has led to common misconceptions, for instance, that deaf people are mentally and emotionally disabled, and therefore unable to live productive lives. Of course, this is not true. People who cannot hear are as intelligent and as emotionally stable as members of the general population.

Unawareness also causes some hearing people to treat deaf people differently or to ignore them in social situations. This can make deaf people feel misunderstood and isolated. Elizabeth knows these feelings but prefers to emphasize the positive:

> There are many things that I would like to tell hearing people. Deaf and hard of hearing people don't want to be isolated; we want to be treated fairly. We want to be part of the world we live in. We may be deaf, but we have a lot to say. . . . Deaf and hard of hearing people are intelligent. We have dreams and ambitions. . . . I disagree with the idea that being hearing impaired is a disability that limits my life.[1]

This profoundly deaf woman leads a very rewarding life as a percussion soloist with the Cincinnati Symphony Orchestra.

Making Informed Decisions

Lack of knowledge about deafness causes problems for the families of hearing-impaired individuals. Although sooner or later all parents face important decisions concerning their children's future, parents of deaf children are confronted with life-changing decisions as soon as hearing loss is detected. These include determining the way the child will communicate, selecting a treatment option, and deciding whether the child will live at home or attend residential schools.

Learning all they can about deafness helps parents to make informed choices. A parent of a deaf child advises: "It's really important for you to . . . educate yourself and find out as much as you can about all the different options out there. . . . I think it is important for you to feel like you read all you can read and you've talked to everyone you can talk to. . . . And so you have some sort of control or power in the situation."[2]

The insensitive behavior of some hearing people toward their deaf peers can cause the latter to feel inferior and socially isolated.

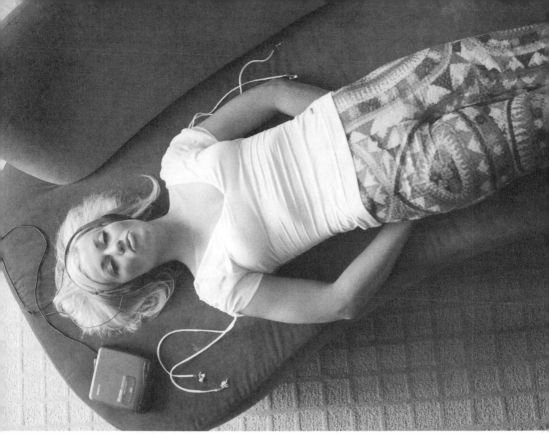

Listening to loud music on a personal sound system can cause significant and permanent hearing loss.

Protecting the Ears

Even those who have no deafness in the family can benefit from learning about noise-induced hearing loss, a hearing impairment caused by exposure to loud noise. According to the National Institute on Deafness and Other Communication Disorders (NIDCD), approximately 30 million Americans are regularly exposed to sound levels that can cause hearing loss. Because noise levels in the United States have risen sixfold in the last fifteen years, ever-increasing numbers of Americans are at risk.

To protect hearing, people can use protective devices such as ear plugs and avoid harmful behaviors such as listening to a personal sound system at loud volume. But many ignore these commonsensible measures. Increased awareness of the ways in which hearing can be endangered can mean the difference between an individual becoming hearing impaired or not. Marianne Schumacher, executive manager of the National Foundation for the Deaf (NFD) of

New Zealand, points out: "If we can learn about what is likely to affect our hearing, take measures to moderate the impact and protect it during the course of our lives then we should still have the majority of hearing well into old age."[3]

Deaf Awareness Week

Learning about deafness is so important that the World Federation of the Deaf, an umbrella organization composed of deaf associations all over the world, organizes an annual Deaf Awareness Week. People in Canada, Great Britain, the United States, Jamaica, Australia, Kenya, and 144 other nations have the opportunity during Deaf Awareness Week to attend events and exhibits that educate the public about deafness. For example, people can meet and talk to many famous and distinguished deaf individuals. By participating in Deaf Awareness Week, the public can learn more about the types and causes of hearing loss and gain awareness of the impact hearing loss has on people's lives.

This knowledge helps the friends and family members of hearing-impaired individuals to make wise decisions and provide more support for their loved ones. It also helps hearing people to better understand and respect deaf people's uniqueness.

Able to Accomplish Anything

Deaf people can do everything that hearing people can do except hear. Their impairment does not limit them, but it does make accomplishing their goals more challenging. Even so, most deaf people do not consider themselves disabled. Instead they regard themselves as different from hearing people due to the distinct ways they compensate for their lost sense.

"People are like stars," Jessica explains. "We have different traits that make us who we are, different strengths and weaknesses, different abilities and inabilities. Deaf and hard of hearing people are no less than people with normal hearing." Learning about deafness forges a bond between hearing and deaf people while helping deaf people to meet their many challenges. Jessica speaks for many when she anticipates a time when this bond will help all hearing-impaired people to "become shining stars."[4]

Chapter 1

What Is Deafness?

DEAFNESS IS THE decreased ability to hear sound. It can affect not only the intensity of the sound a person hears but also whether certain sounds are heard at all. Few people are completely deaf. Most have some residual hearing and can therefore hear some sound. But the amount each person can hear varies depending on the part of the ear that is damaged and the severity of the damage.

In normal hearing, the ear converts sound waves into electrical impulses that are sent to the brain and interpreted as sound. For this sequence to be successfully completed, certain events must occur in a certain order. If anything goes wrong along the chain, deafness can result.

To better understand the hearing process, scientists divide the ear into three parts: the outer, middle, and inner ear. They classify hearing loss by the part of the ear that is damaged.

Conductive Hearing Loss

Deafness due to problems in the outer and middle ear is known as conductive hearing loss. This is because the job of the outer and middle ear is to conduct, or send, sound waves to the inner ear.

Sound waves are formed when something causes air molecules to vibrate. For instance, plucking a guitar string causes the air around it to vibrate. The vibrations are carried through the air to the outer ear where they are absorbed into the auditory or ear canal, an inch-long tube (2.5cm) lined with thin skin and tiny glands. The glands in the auditory canal produce wax, which

11

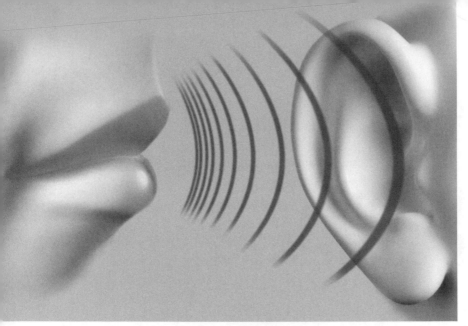

The ears of a hearing person funnel the sound waves of speech to the brain, where they are interpreted as spoken words.

traps dirt and foreign objects that enter the outer ear. A foreign object that is not trapped and proceeds too far down the auditory canal can block some sound waves from passing through the ear. Producing too much ear wax has a similar effect. In either case the impairment caused is similar to what happens when a person places a finger in his or her ear while someone is speaking. Although the voice can be heard, it sounds muted. John, whose outer ear became blocked with ear wax, recalls: "The world just got quieter and quieter. It was like my ear canal was closing up. Everything sounded far away and indistinct."[5]

Once the sound waves pass through the ear canal, they hit a thin sheet of skin known as the eardrum, or tympanic membrane, causing it to vibrate. The vibrations produce motion of the ossicles, three tiny bones located behind the eardrum in the middle ear. In turn, the movement of the ossicles propels the sound waves through a tiny opening, the oval window, which acts as the entrance to the inner ear.

When all goes well, this sequence of events permits sound waves to reach the inner ear. However, if the eardrum is torn or damaged, its vibrations will not be forceful enough to cause the ossicles to move. As a result, the volume of sound the affected person is able to hear is significantly diminished.

Other problems can occur in the ossicles. Sometimes a spongy, bonelike tissue grows over the stapes, the bone closest to the oval window. Over time the tissue hardens and prevents the stapes from moving. In this condition, called otosclerosis, sound waves cannot reach the inner ear. Surgery can usually correct

Sound Conduction

This excerpt from an article in The Encyclopedia of Deafness and Hearing Disorder *by Carol Tarkington and Allen E. Sussman explains how sound is conducted.*

Sound waves move outward in all directions by back and forth movements of molecules through solids, liquids or gases.

Each complete back-and-forth movement (oscillation) is called a cycle, and the number of cycles generated by a sound source every second is known as the frequency. The term "hertz" (abbreviated Hz) represents cycles per second and is named after Heinrich Hertz, a famous scientist who studied sound.

Human ears can detect sounds within a frequency range of 20 Hz to 20,000 Hz; the range of speech lies mostly between 100 and 8,000 Hz. The higher the frequency, the higher the pitch or tone; almost all the sounds we hear are a combination of many frequencies. Sounds used in hearing tests that are only one frequency are called pure tones.

A sound wave's pressure on the surface it contacts is a measure of the sound's intensity, or power. The greater the intensity of the sound waves on a person's eardrum, the louder the sound that is heard. A sound that is barely able to be heard is the threshold intensity.

otosclerosis, but experts do not know why it occurs in the first place. Depending on how completely the stapes is immobilized, otosclerosis can make it almost impossible for a person to hear anything but the loudest sounds.

Another structure in the middle ear, the eustachian tube, regulates air pressure in the ear and is connected to the throat and sinuses. Thus germs from a respiratory infection can travel through the eustachian tube to the middle ear. In this warm environment, infection can take hold, causing swelling and the production of fluids, which makes it difficult for sound waves to pass. Sometimes this happens so suddenly that people who have normal hearing one day can be deaf a few days later. That is what happened to Dave, who recalls: "I lost my hearing suddenly over the space of one week some 20 years ago. On Monday morning my hearing was fine, by Friday I had no hearing."[6]

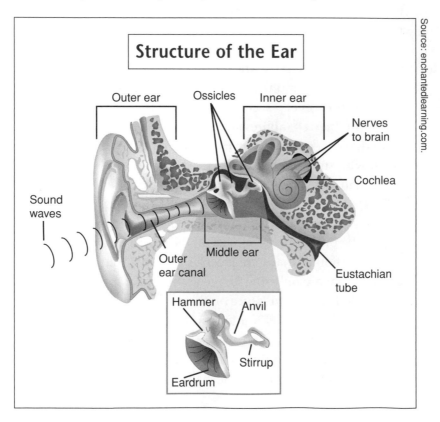

Structure of the Ear

Outer ear   Ossicles   Inner ear

Nerves to brain

Cochlea

Sound waves

Outer ear canal   Middle ear

Eustachian tube

Hammer   Anvil

Stirrup

Eardrum

Sensorineural Hearing Loss

Sensorineural hearing loss results from damage to the inner ear. The job of the inner ear is to convert sound waves to electrical or neural impulses that are carried to the brain and translated into what a person hears: spoken words, music, traffic noises, and so on. When vibrations pass into the inner ear, they enter a snail-like, fluid-filled organ called the cochlea. Each human cochlea contains approximately twenty-three thousand microscopic hair cells that are in contact with the auditory nerve and, hence, are a part of the nervous system.

When sound waves hit the eardrum, resulting vibrations cause the cochlear fluid to move, which in turn makes the hair cells sway back and forth. Half of these cells are stimulated by high-frequency sounds, while the other half are stimulated by low-frequency sounds. Their movement is converted to electrical impulses that are sent along the auditory nerve to the brain, where they are interpreted. Damaged cells will not sway, however, which means that sounds normally conducted by those particular cells cannot reach the brain. As a consequence, both the intensity and the frequency of a person's range of hearing are affected. The greater the number of damaged cells, the more severe the hearing loss. Moreover, unlike the hairs on a person's head, destroyed or damaged cochlear cells do not grow back.

Cochlear hair cells that have lost their sensitivity to sound waves may still produce effects such as ringing, buzzing, or hissing sounds in the ear, a condition known as tinnitus. Although tinnitus does not cause deafness, affected individuals often have trouble hearing environmental sounds over the unwanted noises.

As the difficulties posed by tinnitus suggest, when only some vibrations are transmitted to the brain, the brain has difficulty interpreting the sound it receives. Consequently, an individual with sensorineural hearing loss often perceives sounds as unclear, muffled, and hard to understand. Thus sensorineural hearing loss is usually more serious then conductive hearing loss.

Congenital Deafness

The onset of both conductive and sensorineural hearing loss can occur at any time during a person's life. Some people, however, are born deaf. This disorder, known as congenital deafness, affects three out of every one thousand newborn infants in the United States each year.

Congenital deafness occurs for a number of reasons. Heredity, the primary reason, causes 36 percent of all cases of congenital deafness. Scientists have identified forty mutant genes that may result in deafness. Whether a baby who has inherited one of these genes is born deaf depends on how the defective gene was transmitted. If the inherited gene is dominant, that is, if it carries a trait that is always inherited, only one parent needs to transmit the mutant gene. Thus a baby will be born deaf even if only one parent was a carrier of the mutant gene. Other genes, called recessive genes, will not cause deafness unless contributed by both parents. This means that hearing parents may be unknown carriers of one or more of the recessive genes for deafness.

Deaf parents may or may not carry the genes, since not all deafness is due to genetic causes. Even if one or both parents became deaf genetically, there is no guarantee that their offspring will be deaf. In fact, inherited deafness is unpredictable. Deafness often skips generations; even when it does not, it is common for the same parents to have both hearing and deaf children. A deaf parent of four children provides an example: "Our first child was diagnosed as deaf. . . . I wasn't really surprised when our second child was diagnosed deaf. . . . And then when the third child was diagnosed hearing, it was, like, a shock. . . . Then the fourth child was diagnosed deaf."[7]

Despite the unpredictability of genetic deafness, a dominant gene is likely involved when deafness runs in families. This is because when one dominant gene is transmitted by one parent, the chance that the offspring will bear the trait associated with the gene is 50 percent. Congenitally deaf author Beverly Biderman elaborates: "My father, after all was deaf. . . . So had his mother been deaf, and a brother, and a sister and

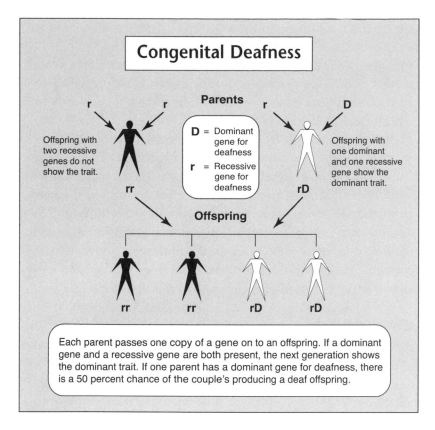

Congenital Deafness

Parents

D = Dominant gene for deafness

r = Recessive gene for deafness

Offspring with two recessive genes do not show the trait.

rr

Offspring with one dominant and one recessive gene show the dominant trait.

rD

Offspring

rr   rr   rD   rD

Each parent passes one copy of a gene on to an offspring. If a dominant gene and a recessive gene are both present, the next generation shows the dominant trait. If one parent has a dominant gene for deafness, there is a 50 percent chance of the couple's producing a deaf offspring.

other relatives. . . . They were all carriers of a dominant gene for deafness that meant there was a 50 percent chance their offsprings would also be deaf."[8]

Viruses and Other Dangerous Substances

Another cause of congenital deafness is prenatal exposure to certain viruses that interfere with the normal fetal development of the hair cells in the inner ear. These include the toxoplasmosis virus, found in cat feces and contaminated soil, and the rubella (German measles) virus. Cytomegalovirus, a form of herpes, is the one that affects the most infants. It causes deafness in approximately four thousand newborns in the United States each year.

Julie's son, Taylor, was one such infant. She recalls: "Taylor had congenital cytomegalovirus. It is a virus that is only harmful to a baby if it is contracted in the womb. . . . Immediately we had questions: What would this mean for Taylor?"[9]

Julie was told that prenatal damage by a virus that attacks the nervous system is permanent and irreversible. Julie learned of her son's condition almost immediately. A hearing test administered before she and Taylor left the hospital showed abnormal results.

Maternal exposure to illegal drugs and certain medications can be just as damaging as viruses to a child's hearing. Repeated maternal use of alcohol is another frequent cause of deafness. In fact, 64 percent of children born with fetal alcohol syndrome, a pattern of abnormality found in children whose mothers are chronic alcoholics, are deaf. Since anything that enters a pregnant woman's body is passed to the fetus through the placenta, it is hardly surprising that 8 percent of all congenital deafness is due to a substance to which the mother was exposed during pregnancy.

Premature Birth

Babies that are born prematurely are also at risk. Ten percent of all cases of congenital deafness occur in persons born before the

These boys suffer from fetal alcohol syndrome, a disease they inherited as a result of their mother's abuse of alcohol. Sixty-four percent of such children are born deaf.

different organs of hearing develop fully. Problems during the birth process that cut off the infant's oxygen supply can also cause congenital deafness. Scientists do not understand how this happens.

Jaundice—a common condition in premature infants, in which the liver does not function properly and produces too much of a substance called bilirubin—also causes deafness. Mary, the mother of a deaf child who was born prematurely, recounts her experience: "Mitch, our first child, was born eight weeks premature. . . . Looking back, we were told, Mitch had several risk factors for hearing loss (high bilirubin counts, low birth weight . . .). We discovered Mitch was deaf at eleven weeks of age."[10]

Acquired Deafness

Most often the onset of deafness occurs after birth. Then the condition is known as adventitious or acquired deafness. Acquired deafness has many causes. In children the most common cause is infection and/or high fever. Common childhood illnesses often accompanied by high fever, such as measles, mumps, chickenpox, and meningitis, can lead to the destruction of the hair cells in the inner ear and cause sensorineural deafness. Some antibiotic medications, such as streptomycin that are used to treat these illnesses can destroy hair cells too. The Gallaudet Research Institute, the largest institute in the world dedicated to the concerns of the deaf, estimates that approximately 21 percent of all deaf persons become deaf from fever or illness. That is what happened to teenage Stephanie: "If you got a fever, you'd probably say, "Bug Whup!" but one little fever changed my life forever. When I was two or three years old, I got a fever that took my hearing. After that, I was confused and upset. I would wonder why I could see my parents' mouths moving, but no sound was coming out."[11]

Similarly, ear infections can lead to deafness. Hearing loss due to swelling and fluid in the middle ear generally disappears when the infection has run its course. But for people who have repeated ear infections, chronic pressure from the fluids can damage the fragile ossicles. This happens most often in babies one year old and under. Their immature eustachian tubes are so

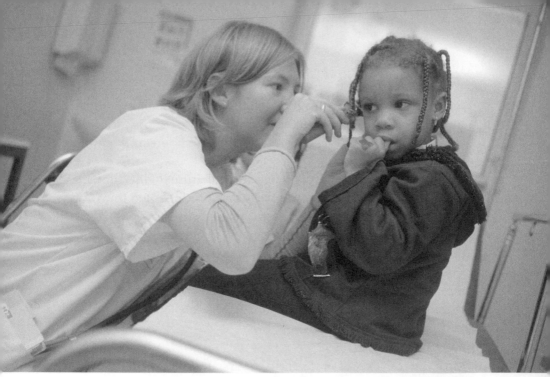

A doctor uses an otoscope to examine a young girl's ear canal. Chronic ear infections are a leading cause of hearing loss in children.

short that throat and nose infections spread easily to their ears. About one in six infants under the age of one suffer from chronic ear infections, which cause 14 percent of all hearing loss. Some experts think that this percentage will rise as more young infants are placed in day-care centers, where contagious infections are common.

Exposure to Loud Noise

Exposure to loud noise is another common cause of acquired deafness. Noise is sound, of course, and the intensity of sound is often measured in units called decibels. For example, intense sound louder than ninety decibels can move the hair cells forcibly enough in the inner ear to damage them. If too many of these cells become damaged, whether due to the shock of one extremely loud noise or to repeated exposure to loud noises, deafness results. Thus hearing loss may be sudden, or the damage can build up over time.

According to the National Institutes of Health, as of April 2004, 10 million Americans were known to have noise-induced hearing loss. And because modern society is extremely noisy, experts predict numbers will grow significantly. High-decibel sound exposure from loud music, surround-sound theaters, Walkman portable audio systems, gardening and farm equipment, power tools, household appliances, airplanes, and highway and city traffic all put people at risk. The National Institute for Occupational Safety and Health reports that 30 million Americans are regularly exposed to hazardous noise that will eventually damage their hearing. "We have become a noisy society and

The Ear and Balance

In addition to allowing people to hear sound, the ear is involved in allowing people to maintain their balance. This is the job of the vestibular system, whose primary organ, the semicircular canal, is located in the middle ear. The semicircular canal is composed of three semicircular tubes.

All three tubes are filled with fluid that moves as the head turns, pressing on sacs at the base of each canal. The sacs contain nerve cells similar to the hair cells in the cochlea. When the fluid presses on the sacs, the nerve cells bend, causing electrical impulses to be sent to the brain. The brain interprets the fluid movement and sends messages to the muscles and eyes to ensure that balance is maintained. Damage to the sacs or the sensory cells causes incorrect information to be sent to the brain. The result is dizziness and other balance problems.

Problems in the vestibular system also lead to Ménière's disease, with symptoms of fluctuating hearing loss, dizziness, and tinnitus. Scientists do not know exactly what causes this disorder of the inner ear, which affects more than 1 million Americans and often leads to profound deafness.

Rock stars like the members of Nine Inch Nails, along with the fans who attend their concerts, are at high risk for hearing loss.

the noise is slowly robbing our hearing,"[12] says Tina Mullins of the American Speech-Language-Hearing Association.

Young people who play certain types of music at high volume, go to noisy dance clubs, and attend heavily amplified concerts are one group at risk. The U.S. Centers for Disease Control and Prevention estimates that at least 5 million Americans between six and nineteen years old already have some hearing loss due to noise. This translates to one out of every eight young people.

People whose work environments are noisy are also at risk. These workers include farmers, musicians, band teachers, factory workers, construction workers, and coal miners. In fact, the U.S. government estimates that 90 percent of all coal miners lose some or all of their hearing by age fifty, and 75 percent of all American farmers have some hearing loss due to their constant exposure to noisy equipment. Ted Madison, the president of the National

Hearing Conservation Association summarizes: "Hearing loss is one of the most common workplace conditions."[13]

Aging

It is well-known that many people lose some or all of their hearing with age. Years of exposure to noise, fevers, and illnesses take their toll on the ears. Conditions that restrict blood flow to the inner ear such as hardening of the arteries or strokes also cause hearing loss. In addition, as people age their eardrums tend to lose elasticity, which inhibits vibration. It is true, as well, that hair cells in the inner ear degenerate gradually over the course of a lifetime.

Thus as people age, their ability to hear decreases progressively. In fact, 75 percent of all Americans seventy-five years old and above have some hearing loss. Although aging is not the primary cause of hearing loss for all of these individuals, its impact is significant. Irene discusses her experience: "I was born with normal hearing but began to lose my hearing around age 50. My hearing loss was progressive. . . . By the time I was 65 . . . I couldn't talk on the phone at all. Even in face-to-face conversations, I couldn't make out what people were saying."[14]

Physical Effects of Deafness

Whether deafness is acquired or congenital, it affects the intensity of the sound heard, as well as its frequency, which creates high or low pitch. Because deafness is often progressive, many people's range of hearing decreases over time. Levels of deafness range from mild to profound. For instance, people with normal hearing can hear sounds at and below 15 decibels. A whisper is about 25 decibels, and a normal conversation is about 60 decibels. Mildly deaf people, also called hearing impaired or hard of hearing, cannot hear sound below a range of 25–40 decibels.

A moderately deaf person cannot hear sounds below 40–70 decibels. This makes it hard to hear music, which is 50–60 decibels. Following normal conversations is also difficult, especially if background noise is competing with speech sounds. Michelle, a moderately deaf teenager, explains: "What hearing I have is enough for me to ask a teacher about a chemistry problem. It is not enough to listen to an album, converse with people in a restaurant, or talk to a classmate on a bus."[15]

Severely deaf individuals cannot hear sounds softer than 70–90 decibels. To put this in perspective, 90 decibels is the loudest sound produced in normal speech. It is also the volume of loud household appliances, alarm clocks, and highway traffic.

The hearing range of profoundly deaf people begins at 90 decibels. Many cannot hear sounds below 100 decibels, the same volume as a thunderclap or a warning siren. Beverly Biderman says that without her hearing aid she "would have heard no speech sounds at all and would have seen a dog's mouth open and close but not heard his bark. I would not even have heard a phone ringing beside me. Nor would I have heard waves crashing as I walked along a beach or leaves rustling underfoot on a trail."[16]

Complicating matters, many deaf individuals have difficulty hearing either high- or low-frequency sounds. The technical definition of frequency is the number of vibrations per second that a sound wave produces. This property is measured in hertz (Hz). The more hertz, the higher the frequency of a sound; a lower number of hertz means a lower frequency. People with normal hearing can hear sounds with frequencies from 20 to 20,000 Hz. Inability to hear high-frequency sounds can make it difficult for even mildly deaf individuals to understand speech. This is because most speech consists of consonants, and almost all consonant sounds are high frequency. Bruce describes how high-frequency hearing loss affected his communication: "I could hear low voices, but without consonants, understanding speech was almost impossible."[17]

Communication Problems

Deafness not only affects people's ability to hear, it also interferes with their speech. Most deaf people have nothing physically wrong with their vocal cords or voices, but their inability to hear their own voice and the voices of others causes problems. The problems are especially severe for prelingually deaf children, that is, children who become deaf before they learn oral language.

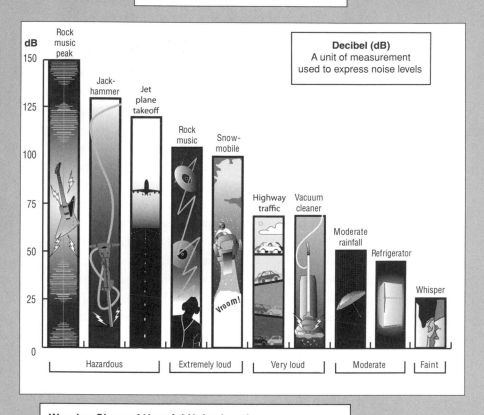

Noise Levels in Decibels

dB

Rock music peak

Decibel (dB)
A unit of measurement used to express noise levels

150

Jack-hammer

125

Jet plane takeoff

Rock music

Snow-mobile

100

75

Highway traffic

Vacuum cleaner

Moderate rainfall

Refrigerator

50

25

Vroom!

Whisper

0

Hazardous | Extremely loud | Very loud | Moderate | Faint

Warning Signs of Harmful Noise Levels
• You must raise your voice to be heard.
• You cannot hear someone two feet away from you.
• Sounds seem muffled or dull after you leave a noisy area.

Since children learn oral language by imitating what they hear and by relating the sounds to the concepts they represent, prelingually deaf children often have difficulties learning to talk. They can see speakers' lips moving but they do not hear any sound coming out; otherwise, the sounds they hear are so muffled and unclear that duplicating them or recognizing their meaning is very hard. Without knowing how speech is supposed to sound, to naturally imitate and learn spoken language is a huge challenge. Deafness expert O. Malone Jr. provides insight: "Deafness is subtle. . . . It imposes few physical limitations. . . . It can cripple neither the mind nor the body, but the ability to use our most elemental and pervasive form of communication, the human voice."[18]

Complicating matters, deaf people who use oral language cannot hear their own voices very well. As a result, even those who become deaf as teens or adults cannot monitor their own speech. They are therefore unable to regulate the volume, rhythm, pitch, inflection, clarity, and pronunciation of their speech. Consequently, their voices and speech may be difficult to understand. Matthew S. Moore and Linda Levitan, the deaf editors of *Deaf Life* magazine, explain: "Good articulation is notoriously difficult to both achieve and maintain. . . . How well can you modulate your voice if you can't hear yourself speaking? You can never really be sure how you sound—the only cues are the expressions on the faces of your listeners. Or comments such as, "Sorry, I can't understand you."[19]

It is clear that a number of factors can cause deafness. And regardless of whether a person is born deaf or becomes deaf later in life, deafness compromises that person's ability to communicate. Hearing loss, and the challenges to communication it presents, can sometimes be diminished or even cured with early diagnosis and proper treatment.

Chapter 2

Diagnosis and Treatment

DIAGNOSING DEAFNESS IS not difficult. However, because hearing loss is often gradual, especially in the elderly, many people are unaware they are losing their hearing and do not seek medical help. In fact, according to Las Cruces, New Mexico, audiologist Lori Kaye, "There are 20 million Americans with hearing loss. But only three to five million have done anything about it. It takes an average of seven years from the time people start losing their hearing to the time that they accept the fact and seek help."[20]

Deafness in infants, too, often goes undetected. Many newborn infants receive hearing screening tests before they leave the hospital. But such tests are not required by federal law and are not universal. Therefore, many children begin life with hearing loss that has not been identified. And since deaf infants cannot tell family members that they cannot hear, it may be months before anyone suspects there is a problem. This usually happens when the infant fails to react to loud noises or exhibits developmental delays in speech. Jamie discovered her son Ryan was deaf when he was one month old: "Our hospital did not offer newborn hearing screening, and with no hearing loss in the family, we felt no need to worry. About a month later, though, we began to wonder. Ryan was never startled when the dog barked; he never turned his head to our voices; he never woke at loud noises in the night."[21]

The Hearing Test

When deafness is suspected, a hearing test is administered by a health-care professional known as an audiologist, who is trained

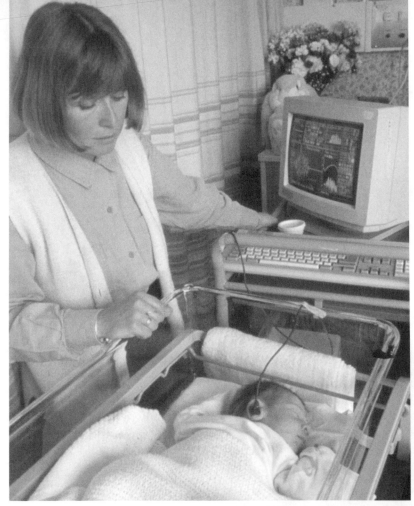

A doctor uses sophisticated equipment to perform a hearing test on a newborn. Without proper testing, deafness in infants can go undetected for years.

to evaluate and treat deafness. Preliminary testing, known as pure-tone audiometry, diagnoses deafness but does not indicate whether the problem is conductive or sensorineural.

The test setup is simple: The person listens through headphones to a series of sounds produced by a machine called an audiometer. All the sounds are different in frequency and intensity. The person being tested pushes a button whenever he or she hears a sound, and the responses are plotted automatically on a graph-like chart. By reviewing the chart, the audiologist can pinpoint the extent of the person's hearing loss. John, whose hearing loss was discovered with a pure-tone audiometry test, describes his experience: "The audiologist . . . told me when I heard a sound to push the button.

A Historical Look at Deafness

Treatment for deafness has changed over the centuries. In ancient times, deaf babies were not given any treatment at all. They simply were not allowed to survive.

Over time, reaction to infantile deafness became less harsh. But the cause of deafness was misunderstood, and so deaf individuals were not treated like other people. For example, in the Middle Ages, it was believed that deaf children were possessed by the devil. Prayers were said for them, and they were given herbs in an attempt to purge the devil from their bodies. When they still could not hear, they were often chained up and locked away for the rest of their lives.

By the seventeenth century, the view that deafness was caused by demonic possession was replaced with the assumption that deafness was a mental disease similar to insanity. Prelingually deaf people spent their lives in mental institutions. Their keepers made no attempt to communicate with them. Indeed, because prelingually deaf individuals were unable to speak intelligibly, it was assumed that they were not only insane but also unable to think or learn. Therefore, there was no point in attempting to communicate with them.

Medical treatment for the deaf was also quite primitive. One popular treatment involved pouring hot wax or hot oil into the deaf person's ear. Ear trumpets, which were the forerunners of hearing aids, were a more useful treatment. This interesting device was shaped like a horn with a small open end that was placed in the ear, and a large round open end for catching sound. Although an ear trumpet was in no way as effective as a hearing aid, it did help amplify the sound that entered the ear.

Then I heard a series of tones. As a listener, I didn't know what I was missing. I consistently missed the high-frequency tones."[22]

Other Tests

If the pure-tone audiometry indicates hearing loss, another test called a bone oscillating test is administered. It determines whether the hearing loss is sensorineural. This test begins by placing a little box connected to an audiometer over one of the person's mastoid bones, which are located inside the skull directly behind each ear. The box vibrates when sound is produced. Because bone can conduct sound, the vibrations should pass from the skull directly into the inner ear. Once again the person being tested is instructed to push a button to signal whenever he or she hears a sound. Since sounds are sent directly to the inner ear, if the person fails to signal, the audiologist knows that the problem is sensorineural.

Still another test is used for infants too young to understand instructions. This test, known as the otoacoustic emissions test, measures emissions that are normally produced by the inner ear when hair cells sway in response to sound. A tiny probe that contains a microphone and a speaker is placed in the infant's ear. The speaker produces a sound at the level of normal speech. The probe records the emissions from the inner ear. If the number of emissions produced is abnormally small, hearing loss is indicated.

Examining the Ear

Once hearing loss is diagnosed, an audiologist, family doctor, or an otologist (a doctor who specializes in treating the ear) administers the ear examination to help pinpoint the cause of the problem. This is important because some conductive hearing disorders can be cured with proper treatment.

The outer ear is visually inspected with an otoscope, a small medical instrument equipped with a light and a magnifying glass. By viewing the ear through the otoscope, a physician or audiologist can diagnose such conditions as an ear infection, excessive ear wax, or a tear in the eardrum.

An instrument that resembles an otoscope, called a tympanometer, is used to diagnose problems in the middle ear. A tympanometer

A physician uses an otoscope to examine the outer ear of a teen patient for signs of infection, wax buildup, or eardrum damage.

contains a tiny vacuum pump, and when the probe is inserted into the outer ear, the pump changes the air pressure in the ear. Like sound, air pressure of different intensities causes the ossicles to vibrate at different speeds. The tympanometer measures these vibrations. Abnormally low measurements indicate otosclerosis.

Treatments That Restore Hearing Loss

Many forms of hearing loss can be cured. For example, antibiotics will eliminate most ear infections. To remove ear wax, doctors insert a special syringe filled with warm water into the ear canal. The surge of water washes the wax out.

Like a cut or scratch, a tear in the eardrum usually heals on its own. If not, a minor surgery called tympanoplasty is prescribed. A surgeon seals the tear with a small piece of skin usually taken from somewhere on the patient's body. With the skin graft sealing the hole, the eardrum can vibrate normally and the patient's hearing is restored.

Surgery also cures otosclerosis. In the procedure known as a stapedectomy, the surgeon removes the damaged stapes bone and

replaces it with an artificial bone. The surgery, in which either local or general anesthesia is administered, is done through the ear
canal. First the surgeon folds back the eardrum. Then with the
help of an operating microscope, the surgeon cuts loose the stapes
with laser and inserts the artificial bone in its place. The whole re-
pair procedure takes about forty-five minutes, and patients can
resume their daily life immediately. The operation restores hearing in 90 percent of all patients, but it does have its dangers. Although complications are rare, the procedure can cause facial
paralysis, and for unknown reasons, sensorineural hearing loss.

Otosclerosis can recur when spongy growth re-forms on the artificial bone and immobilizes it. Some patients experience recur-

*This Chinese girl wears a hearing device to amplify sounds in order to expand
her limited range of hearing.*

rence in a matter of months. Others retain their hearing for decades. Harriet, a psychologist, had good results from her stapedectomy: "I became aware that I could not hear what my clients said to me if they were on my left side. . . . As a result, I had a stapedectomy in my left ear. For another twenty years, I enjoyed excellent hearing."[23]

Hearing Aids
For patients with recurring otosclerosis and those with sensorineural hearing loss, a hearing aid is another option. This electrical device can improve a person's range of hearing significantly by amplifying sound. But the sound still must pass through the damaged cochlea; therefore, the function of the inner ear will not be restored completely. A deaf woman explains: "Simply putting on a pair of hearing aids is not a cure for hearing loss. Although hearing aids amplify sound in the environment, they don't help you compensate for the difficulties that result from hearing loss."[24] Despite these drawbacks, by increasing the intensity of sound entering the ear, hearing aids allow people to hear more than they would without them.

A Microphone, an Amplifier, and a Receiver
There are many types of hearing aids. A behind-the-ear hearing aid is hooked onto the external ear. An inside-the-ear hearing aid is inserted into the ear canal. Whether a person needs one or two hearing aids depends on the severity of the hearing loss, and whether the loss is in one ear or both.

All hearing aids consist of a microphone, an amplifier, and a receiver. The microphone receives sound from the environment and sends it to the amplifier, which makes the sound louder. The amplified sound then goes to the receiver, which further intensifies the sound. The enhanced sound is then transmitted through the ear canal to the eardrum.

Hearing aids have other components. A volume control allows hearing-aid wearers to adjust the intensity of the sound, and a battery supplies electrical energy to the device. Behind-the-ear hearing aids also have an ear mold, a snugly fitting plastic insert that fits in the ear canal and is attached to the receiver with clear plastic tubes. Sound from the receiver passes through the tubes to the ear mold, which conducts the sound into the ear. Inside-the-ear hearing aids do not need an ear mold because the hearing aid itself does the job of the ear mold.

Custom Fitting

Ear molds and inside-the-ear hearing aids are custom-made to fit the shape of the patient's ear. They must be comfortable. At the same time they must fit tightly so they cannot slip. If the fit is too loose, their movement lets sound escape, which causes feedback. On the other hand, if the fit is too tight, soreness and irritation can occur.

An ear mold or inside-the-ear hearing aid can be custom fitted for patients as young as two months. The whole procedure takes about twenty minutes and is painless. First an audiologist takes an impression of the ear canal. A small foam block inserted in the ear acts as a seal and keeps the substance used to make the impression from leaking into the middle ear. Next the audiologist injects a gel-like substance into the patient's ear. The material is left to set for a few minutes and then is carefully removed. The result is an exact replica in size and shape of the patient's ear canal. The impression is sent to a hearing-aid manufacturer who uses it to customize a hearing aid or ear mold that fits perfectly in that patient's ear.

Different Types of Hearing Aids

Hearing aids differ widely in size, shape, and color. Usually the color is similar to that of the wearer's skin, but hearing aids can be made in every color of the rainbow depending on what the wearer prefers.

Size also varies. The smallest are no bigger than a thumbnail. Generally the more severe a person's hearing loss, the larger the amplifier must be and, therefore, the larger the hearing aid. Large inside-the-ear hearing aids completely fill the ear canal, while large behind-the-ear aids equal the length of the exterior ear.

Operating systems are not all alike either. Hearing aids can be analog or digital. Analog hearing aids, in use for forty-five years,

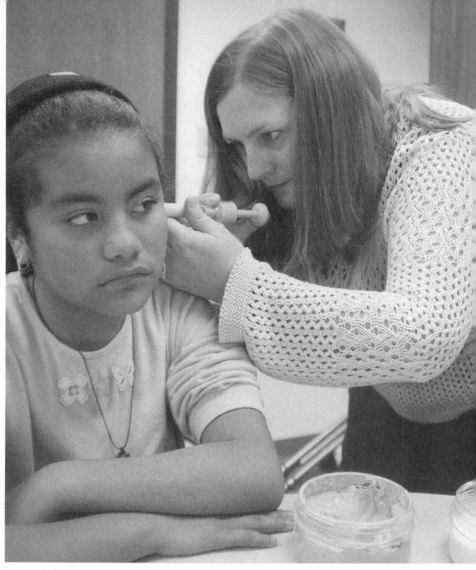

An audiologist makes an impression of a hearing-impaired young woman's ear canal before fitting her with a custom-made hearing aid.

amplify all sound, including background noise. This can make it hard for the user to distinguish between wanted and unwanted sound. As a result, in a noisy environment such as a city street, a busy office, or a restaurant, homing in on a conversation may prove challenging. A deaf woman notes the main disadvantage of analog devices: "These devices amplified all sounds and noises in my environment. There were many times I would become frustrated because I was unable to distinguish voices above background noise."[25]

Digital hearing aids, introduced in 1996, help solve this problem. Digital hearing aids contain a computer chip that is programmed to analyze the sound environment and adapt the amplification accordingly. By pressing a button on the hearing aid, the listener can instruct it to muffle background noise while amplifying speech. This feature helps listeners to better focus in on what is being said. Ten-year-old Nichole explains the benefit of her digital hearing aid: "I was at the school waiting at the bus stop and there were girls talking and I could join in. I've never been able to do that before."[26]

Adjustment

It takes time to adjust to a hearing aid. Some people manage in a few days; others need months. Some people never adjust. For example, those used to a quiet world find the loudness of the

This pair of digital hearing aids can process sounds much more precisely than traditional analog hearing aids.

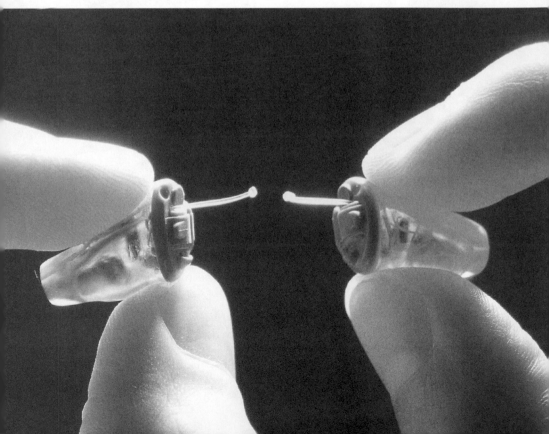

sounds they hear through a hearing aid discomforting. Author John Burkey explains:

> People who try hearing aids often experience a rude shock: they suddenly hear everything. Sure they hear the person they are listening to, but that is not all they hear. They hear the furnace and the refrigerator running, faucets dripping, hinges squeaking, wind blowing, birds chirping, dogs barking and much more. At first, all these sounds are distracting. . . . This initial reaction to noise is a hurdle that most hearing aid users have to overcome. [27]

In addition, the brain must adjust to hearing and processing new sounds. People need a learning period to be able to identify unfamiliar sounds. "Getting a hearing aid is not like putting on a pair of glasses and immediately having your problem corrected," says audiologist Lori Kaye. "It takes time and patience to become aware of sounds you haven't heard." [28]

Despite these obstacles, a hearing aid can greatly improve the ability to hear, and in so doing enhance a person's life. A hearing-aid wearer summarizes the challenges and benefits: "I have been wearing my . . . hearing aids for nine months and my brain is still adjusting to the sounds and experiences that have been missing in my life. Because of these hearing aids life has become a more colorful place in which to live." [29]

Cochlear Implants

For profoundly deaf people with sensorineural hearing loss, a cochlear implant is an option. This hearing device is surgically implanted in the inner ear. It does not cure deafness, but it helps people to hear a clearer, wider range of sound.

A cochlear implant works by converting sound to electrical impulses that are sent directly to the brain. Unlike a hearing aid, which amplifies sound and transmits it to the damaged inner ear, a cochlear implant bypasses damaged hair cells. It takes over the job of the damaged cells by using an array of twenty-two electrodes implanted in the cochlea. This design offers more help to people with sensorineural hearing loss than a hearing aid does.

However, implant effectiveness varies from patient to patient, and even at best it cannot duplicate normal hearing.

A cochlear implant consists of external and internal parts. A tiny microphone, a transmitter, and a speech processor make up the external components. The microphone is worn behind the ear like a hearing aid. It picks up environmental sounds and sends them via a connecting wire to the speech processor.

The speech processor is a computer about the size of a deck of cards. Users wear it behind the ear, hooked onto a waist band, or tucked into clothing. It converts the sound it receives into electrical impulses of different frequencies and volume.

The electrical impulses are sent back up the wire to the transmitter, which is worn on one side of the head right above the ear. It fastens magnetically to the receiver implanted under the skin, in the mastoid bone. No bigger than a quarter, the transmitter sends the electrical impulses across the skin to the receiver.

The receiver picks up the signals and transmits them through a wire to the electrodes inside the cochlea. Each electrode is programmed to receive signals of a specific range of frequency and pitch. The electrodes stimulate the auditory nerve, which carries the electrical signals to the brain, where they are interpreted as sound.

The Surgery

Because the inner ear is not easily accessible, cochlear-implant surgery is complex. The process takes two and one-half hours and is performed under general anesthesia. When the patient is asleep, a surgeon makes a small incision in the mastoid bone behind the middle ear, drills a small hole into the bone, places the receiver in the hole, and secures the site.

Next the surgeon makes another hole. This time it is in the oval window. The electrodes are threaded through this hole and placed in the cochlea area. Finally all the incisions are closed. Orlando, Florida, surgeon Patrick Antonelli describes the procedure: "We use an operating microscope to sneak behind the brain down behind the ear canal and find the nerves to face and taste. We go between those two nerves and put electrodes into a hole in the cochlea, the inner ear. We secure the receiver, where we send signals behind the ear."[30]

Getting Hooked Up

It takes at least a month for patients to heal from cochlear-implant surgery. Then the external equipment is hooked up. At the initial stimulation session, the cochlear implant is activated for the first time. After the audiologist has attached the external equipment, a computer produces a series of beeps, which the audiologist uses to test the listener's hearing. One cochlear implantee, former Miss America Heather Whitestone McCallum, recalls:

> An audiologist . . . hooked a hearing-aid size speech processor on my ear. Behind my ear, she placed a transmitter coil which

Heather Whitestone McCallum, who uses a cochlear implant to hear, makes the sign for "I love you" after she is crowned Miss America 1995.

fastens magnetically to the implant under the skin. . . . Then she started to test the implant, clicking out sounds from her laptop. "Anything?" she asked, but I shook my head, no. Then, faintly, I began to hear a series of beeps. "Yes, a little bit," I said. "Now a little stronger."[31]

Next the audiologist checks to see whether the listener can hear natural sounds such as a hand clap, a bell ringing, or a human voice. In many cases sounds seem distorted and overly loud at first. Indeed many patients are disappointed that they cannot hear normally as soon as the device is turned on. As with hearing aids, it takes time for the brain to adjust to hearing sounds and to learn how to interpret them. To help make this process easier, the audiologist adjusts the speech processor to suit the individual in a procedure called mapping. Mapping is an essential and ongoing activity, since different people require different amounts of stimulation to hear best with the implant. As individuals become more accustomed to hearing, the audiologist continues to fine-tune the processor.

Even with frequent mapping sessions, individuals must focus on every new sound they hear to train their brains to remember the sounds and what they represent. It can take months or even years to learn to hear and identify individual sounds and voices. Neal, an implantee who became deaf at age seven, explains: "It's like striking a match in a dark room, rather than switching on a bright light. It seems like every week, I hear something different. Or I recognized a sound I haven't categorized before."[32]

Problems Can Arise

Not all cochlear-implant patients regain the same level of hearing. Many people regain 50 percent of hearing in the implanted ear but the results are negligible in others. Experts do not know exactly why this is so, and there is no way to predict who will be helped most. But the majority of cochlear implants help the wearer to better connect with his or her environment.

As with all surgeries there are risks. For example, the insertion of the electrodes can damage working hair cells, lessening

The Cochlear Implant Controversy

The use of cochlear implants in children is controversial, especially among members of the Deaf Community. Members of this community are people who use sign language to communicate. These people do not view deafness as a disability. Instead they see deafness as a cultural affiliation, and the use of sign language as an alternative lifestyle. They say that because cochlear implant surgery is complex and the implants are permanent, it should only be done on adults who understand what the surgery entails and how it will affect their lives. They point out that damage to the cochlea as a result of inserting the electrodes can destroy a person's residual hearing. Thus children with cochlear implants might not be able to benefit from possible cures for sensorineural deafness developed in the future.

Moreover, most children with a cochlear implant never learn sign language. This keeps them from being part of the Deaf Community. And the idea that deafness must be corrected delivers the message to these children that deaf people are broken and need to be mended.

Other people disagree. They say cochlear-implant surgery should be done early because language acquisition is easiest during the first three years of life. If people wait until they are adults to have a cochlear implant, they miss out on critical speech and language development.

Having a cochlear implant, these people say, makes it easier for deaf children to function in a hearing world, and helps hearing parents develop closer bonds with their child because they can communicate with each other more easily.

In the end, it is up to the families of deaf children to weigh the advantages and disadvantages, and make an informed decision based on what is best for their child.

or destroying the implantee's residual hearing. That is why cochlear implants are never placed in both ears. Moreover, for unknown reasons, the implant appears to put children at risk of developing meningitis, a potentially lethal disease. According to the Centers for Disease Control, children with a cochlear implant are thirty times more likely to develop the disease than other children.

Despite these problems, many recipients of a cochlear implant say their lives have changed for the better. Teenage Jessica puts it this way: "Cochlear implants are not automatic cures for hearing loss, but the cochlear implant I received has worked wonders for me."[33]

Indeed, treatment for hearing loss can work wonders for many people. Some treatments can cure hearing loss. Other treatments can increase a person's range of hearing and thereby change his or her life forever.

Chapter 3

Many Ways to Communicate

HEARING LOSS MAKES it difficult for people to understand what is going on around them and to be understood by others. Therefore, in addition to improving range of hearing, treatment for deafness involves improving the ability to communicate. This is accomplished in many ways. Speech and auditory-verbal therapies (AVT) help individuals to communicate orally. Speechreading, often called lipreading, helps people to use their eyes to "hear." Sign language allows communication with anyone, deaf or not, who knows how to sign. It also provides a cultural bond among users of this visual language.

Experts on deafness do not agree on which method is best. That may be because no one method is right for everyone. The severity of an individual's deafness, the age when he or she becomes deaf, and the age when communication training begins all affect how successful any method will be. As one parent of a deaf child says: "There's no right or wrong. There's no answer. It's a guessing game."[34]

Auditory-Verbal Therapy

A deaf child's family usually decides whether the child should be trained to communicate orally or visually. If the choice is oral language, the child will likely undergo auditory-verbal therapy. Melissa and her husband made this decision for their young daughter: "It was very important to us that she learn to communicate orally so that she could be a part of the mainstream. . . . We began working with our Auditory-Verbal therapist as soon as she was hooked up [to a cochlear implant] and never looked back." [35]

Auditory-verbal therapy is based on the premise that deaf children cannot learn to communicate orally unless they are made aware of sounds and their various meanings. It uses structured lessons, songs, games, pictures, and toys to help children learn to listen, identify sounds with objects, and use the sounds to produce words. For example, in one activity, the audio-verbal therapist shows the child a toy car and repeatedly says, "That's a car. It goes b-b-beep." Then as part of a game, the therapist puts the car in a box with other toys and asks the child to find the car that goes b-b-beep. If the child succeeds, he or she has connected the sound with the object.

This profoundly deaf child uses a cochlear implant and is learning to speak with the help of audio-verbal therapy.

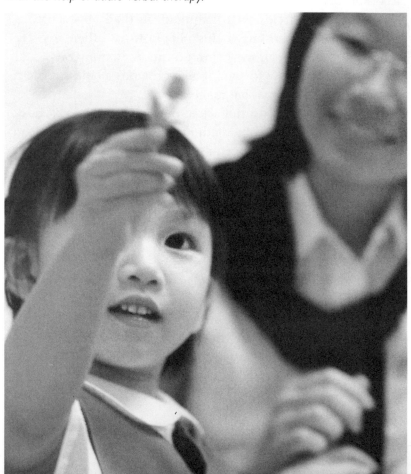

At home the parent repeats the activity as often as possible. Many children soon start repeating the initial "b" sound, which is purposely exaggerated so the child can hear it better, and use it to form words and then sentences.

Frequent Training

AVT sessions are usually held at least once a week and last about an hour and a half. Parents are given daily activities to work on at home with the child. Depending on the child's age, attention span, and listening skills, such activities may include drawing attention to sounds, developing early vocabulary, and practicing simple conversations.

Laurie describes the different activities she and her daughter Annie, a toddler, participated in:

> Under the therapist's guidance we learned to play sound games using tongue-clacking for a horse, "meow" for a cat . . . and so on. . . . Every time Annie responded to a sound, we were to reward her with the appropriate toy. We were also encouraged to show Annie the source of regular household sounds like the telephone, running water, and the doorbell. As with any baby, we were reminded to keep a running commentary of everything we are doing when Annie is in the room. Basically, our job was to bombard her with language and keep it fun.[36]

Effectiveness of AVT

Successful auditory-verbal therapy calls for a strong commitment of time and energy. Moreover, the greater the range of hearing, the more effective AVT is. This is because it is easier to train a person to attend to sound if he or she does not have to struggle to hear it. Consequently, AVT works best for children with moderate hearing loss, or combined with a cochlear implant or a hearing aid. These devices make sound more accessible to the listener, thus helping to increase a severely or profoundly deaf person's chance of success.

The age of the client also influences the therapy's effectiveness. This is because failing to use the auditory nerve to listen to sound causes it to atrophy. That means that the longer the nerve is not put to use, the less able it is to do its job. Furthermore, language acquisition occurs most easily during the first five years of life. So the older the client, the more difficult it becomes to learn language. Despite these drawbacks, AVT has helped many deaf children, like three-year-old Comrie, to develop excellent listening and oral communication skills. His mother is extremely pleased with the progress the boy made with AVT: "When Comrie so emphatically scolds our dog for going on the road, or praises his brother for eating all his dinner, we know we made the right choice for our child, who was now very verbal."[37]

Speech Therapy

Speech therapy is another treatment that helps deaf individuals to communicate orally. Trained professionals, known as speech pathologists or therapists, instruct clients of all ages on how to position their mouths and tongues, and how to control their voices and breathing to produce clear speech. Speech therapy helps prelingually deaf children develop the skills they need to speak intelligibly, as well as assisting people who once could hear improve the quality of their speech. These postlingually deaf individuals often forget particular sounds as their period of deafness lengthens, and then they lose confidence in their speaking ability. Speech therapy helps them to become more aware of their speech.

Since the goals of speech therapy are wide-ranging, speech therapists develop individualized programs to meet each client's specific needs. In order to do this, the therapist uses a large variety of activities. Most take advantage of the client's sight to help them learn how to form sounds and words.

For example, to show how speech sounds are made, therapists model particular lip and tongue movements for clients to imitate. One therapist may do the modeling with her own mouth. Another may show the client flash cards of the mouth and tongue to provide images for his client to study. There are computerized

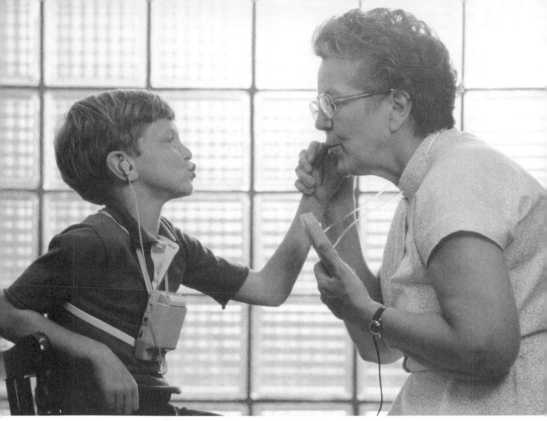

Using sight, touch, and mimicry, a speech therapist teaches a deaf boy how to articulate intelligible sounds.

methods as well. For example, both the therapist and the client may wear special sensors on their mouths that are connected to a computer to set up a feedback loop. When the therapist says a sound or word, an image is formed on the computer that illustrates the position of the tongue. The client repeats the sound until the image on the computer monitor matches that of the therapist's. Other computer programs resemble video games in which clients win when they produce a correct sound or speak at an acceptable volume.

Still other computer programs let individuals see the quality of their speech through the use of a device called a laryngograph. Instead of measuring the range of a person's hearing, like an audiometer, the laryngograph measures the pitch, breathiness, and intensity of speech. It displays the data in the form of a graphlike illustration on a computer monitor. Clients compare their own graph to that of the therapist, with the goal of duplicating the therapist's measurements.

The History of Sign Language

In 1760 Charles-Michel de l'Epée, a French priest, established a school for the deaf in Paris. De l'Epée was one of the first people to believe that the deaf could learn. The school was the first in the world that taught only deaf children.

Sign language was the primary form of communication at the school. However, at the time there was no formal system of sign language. Deaf people signed among themselves using signs that they had developed. But without a formal language, signs and their meanings varied widely among the deaf. This made it difficult for deaf people to communicate with each other. De l'Epée collected the signs that his students used and invented new signs. From this, French Sign Language was born.

French Sign Language found its way to the United States forty-four years later, in 1816, when Thomas Hopkins Gallaudet, an educator and clergyman, went to France to visit de l'Epée's school.

In Paris, Gallaudet met Laurent Clerc. Clerc, who was deaf, was a teacher in the French school. Gallaudet convinced Clerc to return to America with him. In the next year, through the use of gestures, finger spelling, and writing, Clerc, who could not speak, taught Gallaudet French Sign Language. Together the two men translated French signs into American English.

In 1817 they opened the first signing school for the deaf in the United States in Hartford, Connecticut. As in France the students had their own natural sign language. Gallaudet incorporated these signs with signs derived from French Sign Language. The result was American Sign Language, which made it possible for deaf people throughout the United States to communicate easily with each other.

As with auditory-verbal therapy, speech therapy does not work for everyone. It is most effective in helping postlingually deaf people build on their early experience with language. Still, with the help of speech therapy, many deaf people become fluent oral-language speakers and are able to communicate quite effectively. Lewis, a successful user of techniques learned in speech therapy, has this to say: "Although I do not think about it much, I do take pride in the fact that I communicate orally. It's unquestionably an achievement to be able to communicate with hearing people on something close to their terms."[38]

Sign Language

Although learning to communicate orally is a profound achievement, the deaf speaker's voice may sound much different from a hearing speaker's. In his autobiography, deaf journalist and two-time Pulitzer Prize–nominee Henry Kisor recalls that after years of speech therapy, "my speech had become quite intelligible, though nobody would mistake my breathy monotone and foggy articulation for the voice and speech of a normal hearing child."[39] In fact, years later when Kisor took up flying, one of the problems he faced was the ground personnel's inability to understand his speech over the airplane's radio.

Such speech differences can be frustrating and embarrassing for both the speaker and the listener. In addition, even with the help of speech or auditory-verbal therapy, many profoundly prelingually deaf children find it difficult to learn oral language. Their lack of experience with language prevents them from interacting fully with family members. This blocks progress because interaction with language is integral to acquiring it. Therefore, they often enter oral programs with no linguistic base to make sense of the world. For one deaf man, the experience was disastrous: "My parents didn't sign at all. . . . They put me in an oral program, and it just didn't work because I had no language. . . . I was completely lost."[40]

For prelingually deaf children, there are so many obstacles on the road to acquiring oral language that it may take years before they can communicate effectively. Even when they do speak, they are often delayed in vocabulary development. This can make connecting with others difficult, so many parents seek an alternative to AVT and speech therapy.

Sign language is the easiest way for prelingually deaf children to acquire language. This is because learning sign language calls on learners to use their strongest sense, rather than their weakest, to attain proficiency in language. That may be why an estimated 90 percent of all prelingually deaf adults use sign language as their primary language. A mother of a prelingually deaf child explains her choice of this mode of communication:

> We wanted something with a 100% guarantee method of success, and sign language was the only guaranteed method. We wanted immediate success. And what I kept hearing about pursuing the oral method without reliance on signs was so time intensive it might take months and months before our child uttered a sound. My child was only 3 months old and her loss was so profound. Sign was my success route.[41]

A Visible Language

Sign language is visible language. Instead of the vocal cords, it uses the hands, fingers, facial muscles, and body language to communicate ideas. These visual symbols transmit ideas to the brain through the eyes rather than the ears.

Signs can represent single words or ideas. Many signs use visual imagery for signing an idea, such as using the hands in a sweeping motion to form whiskers on the face to mean "cat." Signs also use actions like giving a hug to mean "love."

In addition to using their hands, some signers use finger spelling to help them express words, ideas, and proper nouns that there are no signs for. Finger spelling uses the fingers to represent the letters of the alphabet. Using twenty-six different finger positions, some of which exactly represent the printed letter, finger spellers literally spell out words with their fingers. The person the finger speller is speaking to interprets the spelling as a whole unit, the way readers understand written words on a page, rather than letter by letter.

Hands and fingers are not the only body parts sign-language speakers use to communicate. Signers use their whole body expressively to convey meaning, attitude, and vocal inflection. For example, raising an eyebrow indicates a question, a nostril twitch indicates agreement, and a shoulder shrug means "I don't know."

A Popular Language

Over five hundred thousand people in the United States use sign language. This makes it one of the most widely used languages in America. It is also utilized throughout the world. Like oral languages, sign language is not universal. Each country has its own sign language, and even within a country, there are regional differences. Furthermore, like speakers of oral language, every signer has his or her own "voice," or unique style of signing. Sign language also contains slang, humor, rhymes, and word play just like any other language.

A volunteer from NASA reads aloud to a class of hearing-impaired children as their teacher translates the story into sign language.

People in the United States use American Sign Language (ASL). Besides being a visual language, it differs from standard English in many ways. For instance, unlike standard English, in which the common word order of a sentence is subject–verb–direct object, word order in ASL changes depending on what word the speaker wants to emphasize. Usually the speaker states the topic of the conversation first, and then elaborates on it. For example, rather than saying "That was a great party last night," as a speaker would in standard English, an ASL user might sign, "Party, wow! last night."

Another important difference is that ASL has no articles or passive verbs. It is an active language. In addition, sign language has no written form. Therefore, besides learning ASL, most sign-language speakers also learn to read and write standard English.

A student signs one of the five meanings attached to the phrase "made up." ASL rarely translates word-for-word into standard English.

Signed English

Signed English is a form of sign language that, unlike ASL, follows the same word order as spoken English. Developed in 1973, it frequently combines manual gestures with oral speech as a way to clarify what is being said for postlingually deaf people.

Unlike ASL, signed English is not an actual language. It is more of a manual code that translates English to visual language. The words used in signed English match thirty-five hundred of the most commonly used words in the English language. Finger spelling is used to spell out words not included in the thirty-five hundred. In addition, it uses fourteen special signs known as sign markers. These stand for the most common grammatical changes to nouns, indicating whether a word is singular, plural, or possessive.

Signed English is easier for hearing people to learn than ASL because it follows the speech patterns of standard English. It is often used in schools to help ASL signers build English language skills and improve their ability to read and write English. But for everyday conversation, most signers prefer ASL. It is more expressive and clearer. This is because in signed and oral English a word can have more than one meaning, but in ASL a different sign is used for each meaning of a word. So ASL users sign *'feet'*, the measurement, and *feet*, the body part, differently, but signed English speakers do not.

Learning Sign Language

Individuals learn sign language in the same manner they learn any language. Children who grow up in signing homes learn to sign naturally, just as hearing children who grow up in hearing homes learn to speak. In fact, experts say that all babies sign, to some degree, even before they start talking. For example, hearing and deaf toddlers both attempt to communicate with facial movements and hand gestures. They point, make faces, wave good-bye, and push unwanted hands away. Therefore, it is not surprising that deaf infants who grow up in a signing environment usually start signing earlier than hearing babies start speaking intelligibly.

People who grow up in nonsigning homes must be taught to sign. According to the National Association of the Deaf, it takes at least two years for people who study ASL to pick up enough signs to communicate effectively. Speech therapists often teach deaf clients sign language; so do early intervention programs that work with deaf infants and toddlers, and special schools for the deaf. Colleges, community centers, and churches offer courses in sign language for interested hearing people who want to learn the language. In fact, many universities accept ASL to satisfy students' foreign-language requirements.

A Linguistic Community

Using ASL brings signers together. It provides them with a common language in which they can converse easily. In fact, people using ASL can communicate with each other from across a crowded room, or underwater. And because language is such an important component of anyone's background, users of ASL share a unique culture. As a result, deaf people who sign have bonded with each other to the extent of identifying themselves as Deaf, with a capital D to represent being part of a culture. They use the term Deaf Community to designate signing people as opposed to those who communicate orally. Kathryn, a signer, is content: "I don't need sound for communication now. I have a collection of skills and options. . . . I have a social circle that accepts deafness and can communicate with me."[42]

Speechreading

Speechreading, or lipreading, helps people who speak orally or with signs to understand what oral speakers are saying. A speechreader discerns spoken language by focusing intently on the lips, mouth, tongue, and jaws of someone who is talking. The speechreader mentally links the observed movements to the sounds and words that they ordinarily form.

To some extent, most oral speakers, whether hearing or deaf, speechread naturally just to help themselves to hear better. Postlingually deaf individuals often build on this natural ability and become adept speechreaders almost unconsciously as a way to compensate for their hearing loss. That is what happened to Juanita's daughter. Juanita explains: "When my daughter was a little girl she got the mumps and totally lost all hearing in one ear and partial hearing in her other ear. The hearing loss didn't affect her speech because she already could talk. As far as understanding us, she learned to compensate. By the time she started school, her teachers said she had taught herself to read lips."[43]

A Tricky Skill

Speechreading is taught by speech therapists and in special classes in schools for the deaf. But not all deaf people acquire this

Deaf students watch video monitors of speaking mouths in order to learn how to speechread, or lipread.

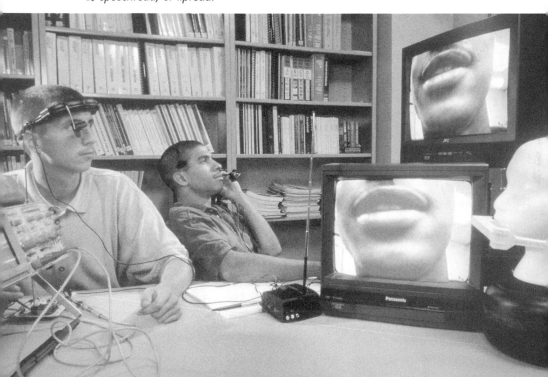

ability. Speechreading is easier for people with a background in oral language. It is more difficult for prelingually deaf signers to learn.

Even excellent speechreaders cannot always understand words by carefully watching speakers. The primary reason is that only one-third of all English sounds are clearly visible on a person's lips. Of those that are visible, half look like and are easily confused with other sounds. For example, the words *chair* and *share* look almost the same; so do the shapes of the sounds of the letters F and V, and B and P. Therefore, speechreading takes a lot of guesswork. Indeed, the name of Henry Kisor's book, *What's That Pig Outdoors?*, is based on what Kisor mistakenly speechread when his son asked, "What's that big loud noise?"

To compensate, speechreaders use context clues, facial expressions, gestures, and body language to help fill in the blanks. Kisor elaborates: "Lipreaders must . . . actively hunt for clues to what is being said. Listening of this kind is extremely hard work. We cannot look out the window briefly to rest our eyes or to digest a piece of information. If we do so, we might miss something important and even lose the thread of the discussion."[44]

Sometimes a speechreader is unable to see a speaker's lips clearly. Circumstances such as poor lighting, facial hair, a hat that overshadows the face, a hand placed over the speaker's mouth, and a face turned away from the listener can make it almost impossible for speechreaders to tell what is being said. In addition, the volume of the speaker's voice is a source of distortion. When people shout their faces change shape, which makes it more difficult to read their lips. Under favorable conditions, though, an experienced speechreader is generally able to carry on a conversation. Kisor says: "As long as the other person faces me, perhaps speaking more slowly than usual and can give me undivided attention, we can connect."[45]

Cued Speech

One way to make lipreading easier is through a visual communication system known as cued speech. In cued speech, oral speakers use eight hand shapes and four hand positions near the mouth

The mother of a deaf high school basketball player signs the coach's instructions to her son during a timeout.

to distinguish between sounds that look alike on the lips. The combination of cues and mouth movement helps clarify what is being said for the speechreader.

Cued speech is not very popular in the United States because both the hearing person and the deaf person must know how to form and read the hand symbols. This system is often taught in schools for the deaf, however, and is widely accepted in Australia and Canada.

What Works Best

Neither experts nor deaf people in general agree on what form of communication best serves the deaf. Many deaf people are comfortable using oral language. Others prefer sign language. Some utilize speechreading when listening to oral speakers, while others do not. Many deaf people combine all possible methods of communication in a system known as Total Communication: They adapt their communication method to whatever is easiest for them and most functional in a particular situation. This means they are likely to sign with deaf friends, speak with hearing friends, and use speechreading in classrooms and similar situations. A parent whose son uses Total Communication puts it this way: "People have to talk, you have to communicate—[you] use any means necessary."[46]

In the end what really matters is that deaf people are able to communicate. The way they do this is an individual decision. It is clear that different methods best serve different people. Some people choose oral communication and others sign language, while still others combine these methods. Fortunately, deaf people today have available a variety of methods of understanding and being understood.

Chapter 4

Living with Deafness

DEAF PEOPLE MUST overcome many hurdles. Difficulty hearing and communicating presents safety issues as well as learning and social problems. Assistive and alerting devices, special services, and the caring support of others help people with hearing loss to adapt to and connect with the world around them. As a result, individuals are better able to meet the challenges they face and live happy, productive lives. Jonathan, a deaf teenager, has this encouraging message: "I gradually . . . learned to adapt and to survive in a world built for people with normal hearing. . . . Each and every one of us is capable of standing on our own two feet."[47]

The Challenges of Daily Living

Performing everyday tasks that are simple for hearing people can be challenging for deaf people. For example, using the telephone is tricky. Hearing-impaired ears receive sound coming through a phone in distorted forms with no visual cues to help clarify what is being said. Therefore, most deaf people cannot hear well enough to understand what a caller is saying. Angela, a deaf woman, recalls: "Using the phone was just too frustrating. I could hear voices, but could not decipher what they were saying, so I just gave it up completely."[48]

Many deaf people cannot hear the phone ring; nor can they hear the doorbell, an alarm clock, oven timer, or warning devices such as a smoke alarm, police or emergency siren, or car horns. This can cause them to feel cut off, dependent on others, and

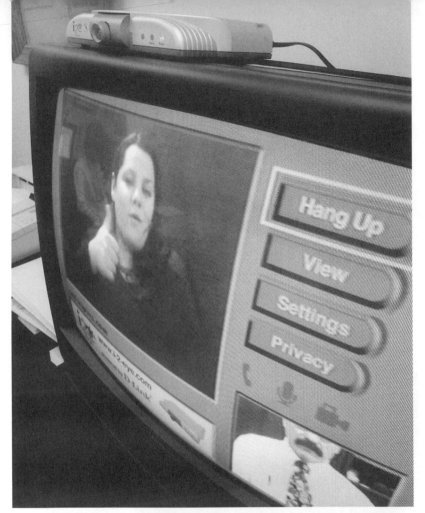

Two deaf people use a cutting-edge video relay system to communicate with each other long-distance.

fearful of the world around them. To cope with these issues, deaf people use a number of assistive devices or tools. Some assistive devices make using the telephone easier. Others provide alternative means of communication. Still other devices alert people to important sounds.

Telephone Aids

Telephone aids, as the name suggests, enable deaf people to use the telephone. A telecommunication device for deaf people known as a TTY, for teletypewriter, allows users to send and receive text messages through regular phone lines. TTYs look like computer keyboards with a small readout panel. Parties to a conversation type in what they want to say, and the words are displayed on the readout panel. When both parties have a TTY they can communicate directly. When only the deaf person has the device, it is necessary to use a relay service in which a human operator reads the text message over the phone to a hearing recipient and transcribes an oral response into text which appears on the TTY screen.

Such service for the deaf has been required by federal law in the United States since 1991. As a result, telecommunication companies must make this equipment available to deaf clients at a low cost. It helps deaf people feel safer and more connected to the world around them. "There are new opportunities and new

A woman types a message over a TTY device during a phone conversation. TTYs and other devices allow deaf people to communicate remotely with others.

technology for all deaf people," Quishauna, a deaf teenager, explains. "They can call each other on TTYs. With TTY and relay services they can call each other as well as their hearing friends, family, businesses, and organizations. They can place emergency calls and contact people anywhere in America."[49]

Technology has made more communication devices available. Many people with hearing loss communicate using Internet chatting, e-mail, and instant messaging with vibrating pagers and BlackBerry devices. They also use a video relay service (VRS), which allows signers to communicate with hearing people via a Web camera connected to the Internet. A caller signs a message, which the camera records and transmits to a sign-language interpreter, who relays a translation of the message to the hearing party.

Closed Captioning
Other technology makes it possible for deaf people to understand the audio part of television programs and movies. Closed captioning, which translates the audio segment of television programs into text that scrolls along the bottom of the screen, helps hearing-impaired people to enjoy themselves and feel a part of the hearing world.

Closed captioning can be prerecorded or presented in real time as a live program is aired. Since 1993 all television sets sold in the United States have been equipped with a device that, when activated, provides captions on the screen. In addition, the National Captioning Institute in Falls Church, Virginia, has captioned more than seven hundred movies and music videos on videotapes for deaf people to enjoy.

Alerting Devices
Mechanisms that alert deaf people to important sounds in their environment include telephones with extra-loud ringers, as well as telephones with signal lights that draw the deaf person's attention to incoming calls. Colored flashing lights connected to doorbells, smoke detectors, and oven timers serve similar functions.

A bed-shaking alarm clock is another ingenious device. The clock is connected to a small vibrator that is placed under a pillow or mattress. The clock may also be connected to a lamp that blinks repeatedly until the alarm is turned off.

Stephanie describes the different devices she uses to cope with the challenges of deafness and to help her feel more secure and independent: "I have some hearing devices to make life easier, like a bed shaker to wake me up, a fire alarm that flashes bright light, and a doorbell that makes all of our lamps flash when someone rings it."[50] Such devices not only make life more convenient but also save lives.

Educational Challenges

Beside these challenges of daily living, deaf children and young adults face additional obstacles at school. Deaf students frequently have trouble understanding what is being said, as well as being understood. Those who are able to use words orally often have a limited vocabulary. Hearing people do not encounter the same stumbling blocks in learning.

Deaf students also may appear to be disruptive and noisy simply because they cannot monitor their own voice levels. Beverly Biderman recalls her early school years:

> I started to get into trouble and seemed to spend a lot of time in detention or out in the hall. I was disruptive (because I did not hear what I was disrupting), and noisy (because I could not monitor the loudness of my voice). My behavior in some cases was inappropriate (because I could not pick up subtle conversation cues to follow fast-paced conversations). . . . Academically, I was doing poorly.[51]

Special Programs That Help

Special services and school programs help hearing-impaired students to meet the challenges they face and succeed academically. Early intervention programs, which begin as soon as deafness is diagnosed, provide support for children with developmental delays and their families. Such programs help children from birth to age six to acquire the communication skills they need. Services include speech therapy, auditory-verbal therapy, sign-language lessons, and home-based tutoring, among other things. These services give deaf children a head start in developing communication proficiency, which makes it easier for them to succeed in school. Jose F. Cordero, the director of the National Center on Birth Defects and Developmental Disabilities, strongly supports these programs: "Early detection

Gallaudet University

Gallaudet University is the only university in the world specifically for hearing-impaired students. Located in Washington, D.C., the university was established in 1864. It has a student body of about twenty-two hundred students, almost all of whom lost their hearing before reaching elementary-school age.

It is not easy to be accepted to Gallaudet. Applicants must pass a rigorous entrance exam. According to *The Encyclopedia of Deafness and Hearing Disorders*, "Of the more than 1,400 students who take the exam, usually only half qualify for admission."

The university offers bachelor's degrees in twenty-six fields, as well as master's and doctorate degrees. Gallaudet's courses are taught by 288 faculty members, one-third of whom are hearing impaired. In addition to serving the deaf, Gallaudet offers a master's degree program for hearing individuals in audiology. It also offers a two-year associate's degree for deaf and hearing people who want to become certified sign language interpreters.

The university's library contains the world's largest collection of materials related to deafness, some of which date back to 1546. The university also runs the Gallaudet Research Institute, which is the largest institute in the world and intervention helps develop vital communication skills that will last a lifetime, and maximizes their potential for positive growth."[52]

Mainstreaming and Its Modifications

Once a deaf child is ready to start school, there are a variety of educational options available. Many deaf children go to neighborhood

dedicated to supporting research into a wide range of issues that concern the deaf.

The National Center for Law and Deafness is also housed and maintained at the university. The center works to meet the legal needs of hearing-impaired individuals, as well as working to eliminate discrimination against the deaf caused by communication barriers.

Gallaudet also maintains the National Information Center on Deafness on its campus. This center provides information on many facets of deafness to the public. It also provides information on the university itself. All in all, Gallaudet University is the largest provider in the world of education, research, and service to the hearing impaired.

Gallaudet University in Washington, D.C., is the world's only university specifically for hearing-impaired students.

schools, where they attend classes with hearing students. This is known as mainstreaming.

Often, deaf students attend classes with their hearing peers for much of the day but also go to special classes where they are taught by an instructor who is trained to work with the deaf and hard of hearing. Here they receive individualized attention and instruction in written English, which is often difficult for signers. They also receive coaching in speaking and listening skills, as well as speech therapy. Mainstreaming is most effective when modifications are established to help deaf students cope with the obstacles their hearing loss presents. Simple strategies can be used to make mainstreaming work. For example, preferred seating near the teacher helps speechreaders in two ways: The students can see the teacher's lips more easily, and they are closer to the source of sound.

Technology for the hearing impaired also provides assistance. Many mainstream classrooms use frequency modulation (FM) systems to make sound more accessible to students with hearing loss. An FM system uses radio waves, which unlike sound waves do not weaken as they travel, to connect teacher and students. Typically the teacher clips a small microphone to his or her shirt close to the source of sound. The teacher's speech is amplified and transmitted as FM radio waves to receivers that students either wear around their necks or stand on their desks. Tiny wires attach the receivers to headphones through which the sound reaches the students' ears with a minimum of background noise.

Even with an FM system, however, many deaf and hard-of-hearing students must speechread to understand everything being said. Problems arise because speechreaders cannot watch the speaker's lips and take notes at the same time. Thus most school systems provide deaf learners with note takers, paraprofessionals who attend classes with deaf pupils and take notes. There is a note taker for each deaf pupil. For signers, a sign-language interpreter may be provided. The interpreter sits beside signers in all of their regular classes and signs what is being said. Michelle, an audiologist and deaf-education expert,

Sitting among his hearing peers, this deaf student is making a joke in his high school calculus class.

describes the services available in the public school system of Las Cruces, New Mexico:

> If students are hard of hearing they qualify for an FM system that they wear in school. The school district provides one for every qualified student. It also provides students, who need it, note takers who attend all their classes with them. Basically, the note taker transcribes information for the student. A sign language interpreter is also available. These services enable deaf students to have the same educational access as hearing students.[53]

Residential and Day Schools

Although mainstreaming works well for many students, it is not for everyone. Even with modifications, some people, especially those who are profoundly deaf, are unable to reach their full learning potential in a regular school environment. For these learners, there are special residential and day schools that emphasize visual learning.

Elementary school students learn basic signs in order to communicate with their hearing-impaired classmate (second from right).

All students in these schools are hearing impaired. Day students usually commute to and from a centrally located school via a school bus. Students live on residential school campuses Monday through Friday and return home on the weekends and holidays. All learners receive the same education as hearing students in neighborhood schools, but the lessons and learning environment are adapted to accommodate young people with hearing loss.

For example, classrooms are equipped with carpets, drapes, and acoustic ceiling tiles to improve sound and reduce background noise. Student desks are usually arranged in a circle facing the teacher, which makes it easier for pupils to speechread and see signs. And because teachers are often deaf too, students have deaf role models to inspire them. Claire Bugen, the superintendent of the Texas School for the Deaf in Austin, explains: "Our environment offers students a community of role models where direct communication access and the accommodations necessary to succeed are available to ensure all children reach their potential."[54]

The main language used in the school is tailored to suit the learners. In some day schools, lessons are presented both orally and visually. This use of the system known as Total Communication ensures that everyone can understand what is being said. In these schools, every student is outfitted with his or her own FM system, and each desk is equipped with a microphone.

Sign language is the primary form of communication in most residential schools. Because the students do not go home at night, these schools are a second home. The deaf children are cared for by adult counselors in dormitories or small cottages, and they eat all their meals in the school cafeteria. After school they participate in clubs and sports such as soccer, basketball, cheerleading, drama club, signing choir, and student government, to name just a few of the many activities. And because residential students may be together for twelve years, many students form lifelong bonds.

In both day and residential schools for the deaf, the primary focus is on developing language skills and literacy. To accomplish this, speech therapy, sign language, and speechreading lessons are part of the daily routine. In addition, computers with specially designed educational software and easily available Internet access give the students the opportunity to use their strongest sense to gather information and improve their language, literacy, and communication skills.

Such programs help deaf learners meet the challenges they face head on and succeed. Bugen notes that schools for the deaf "offer students the unique opportunity to form a specific identity that focuses on strengths and unique talents instead of disabilities, all within an environment of physical and emotional safety."[55]

"Don't Say 'Never Mind'"

Even with the help of special academic programs and assistive devices, hearing loss and differences in the modes of communication result for many deaf people in frustration with and isolation from their hearing peers. For example, attending social gatherings can be trying for people with hearing loss. Fast-paced conversations among multiple speakers are practically impossible for speechreaders to follow. This is because a speechreader cannot watch all of the speakers at the same time and therefore loses

Hearing Dogs for the Deaf

Like assistive devices, hearing dogs provide deaf people with help. Hearing dogs are usually intelligent, small mixed-breed dogs that are rescued from animal shelters and trained as part of special programs sponsored by groups like Dogs for the Deaf.

Training starts with puppies and lasts about one year. It focuses on teaching the dogs to alert a deaf companion to eight sounds: a fire or smoke alarm, a doorbell, a door knock, a telephone, an oven timer, an alarm clock, a baby's cry, or the calling of the deaf person's name. The dogs accomplish this by nudging the humans with their noses or paws and leading them to the source of the sound. If the sound indicates danger, the dogs lie down.

Hearing dogs provide deaf people with help and company. And because hearing dogs do not break or run out of power, they provide deaf people with a sense of independence and security that assistive devices cannot impart.

In an article on the Hearing Dogs for Deaf People Web site, Barbara Bird, a deaf woman, explains how Ceri, a hearing dog, changed her life:

> I was missing so many attempts for people to contact me by phone, at the door, and burnt food became my speciality. That is before I was given my hearing dog, Ceri. These days her little face is the first thing I see in the morning. She jumps up to me when she hears the alarm.

track of what is going on in the conversation. In addition, background noises make focusing on speech difficult.

Rather than call attention to their inability to understand, many hearing-impaired individuals pretend they know what is being said. And even when deaf people admit they cannot follow

It's so much nicer than the vibrating under the pillow! Throughout the day, she gives me the freedom to do whatever I want. . . . Ceri is my helpmate, my friend, my protector—and she's fun! I never envisaged how big a difference she would make to my life.

This partially deaf woman relies on her specially trained canine companion for help in her day-to-day life.

a conversation, they often find themselves excluded. It is not un-common for hearing people to become impatient and refuse to re-peat a statement or translate it into sign language. Jessica, a deaf teenager, advises her hearing friends:

> Don't say, "Never mind!" We know it is frustrating when we don't understand the first time and ask you to repeat, but it is hard on us, too, and if there's one thing we can't stand it's "Never mind." In fact, sometimes we play along, smile, and nod our heads when we don't have a clue what was said! We want to belong. We want to laugh at new jokes and take part in the latest gossip. We're not in another world. We just don't always get it the first time around.[56]

The help of hearing loved ones is very important in ensuring that the deaf people are included in conversations. Close friends and family members become adept at repeating or translating what the hearing-impaired person misses, as well as making sim-ple adaptations that enhance the person's ability to hear. For in-stance, holding social events in well-lit, quiet environments reduces background noise and makes speechreading easier; so does turning off the television or background music during fam-ily meals and visiting restaurants during less busy times.

Getting together in environments with good acoustics also helps. Areas with high ceilings or hardwood floors reflect background noise, while carpeted rooms with low ceilings absorb it. Facing the listener and speaking clearly at a normal volume also makes under-standing what is being said simpler. Sitting as close together as pos-sible and being sure speakers talk one at a time also help. Laurie tells how she and her husband, Glen, educate those who are unsure about communicating with deaf people: "Most people do not know how to deal with a disability. . . . When Glen or I would tell them that they could help by just speaking clearly and a little slower and let him see them speak, it helped everyone."[57]

Getting Help from a Support Group

Connecting with other hearing-impaired people is another way people with hearing loss acquire the tools to meet the challenges they face while decreasing feelings of isolation. Joining a support group gives people an opportunity to interact with others who face similar challenges, share their feelings and experiences, and provide mutual encouragement. In addition, guest speakers inform support-group members on the latest information on hearing loss–related issues.

Support groups are sponsored by organizations such as SHHH (Self Help for the Hard of Hearing). Meetings for people of all ages and degrees of hearing loss are held nationwide. Geri, a hearing-impaired woman, describes her experience: "SHHH . . . turned my life around. I have enjoyed the satisfaction of leading two groups and meeting so many wonderful people along the way who have been an inspiration to me in coping with hearing loss."[58]

Summer Camps

Hearing-impaired children can find camaraderie and support by attending summer camps just for children with hearing loss. Sponsored by universities and service organizations, among others, such camps give deaf and hard-of-hearing children the chance to interact by participating in games and projects tailored to meet their needs.

In one popular activity, campers learn to dance by removing their shoes and feeling the vibrations coming from stereo speakers

These deaf high school students are able to feel the sound vibrations of the music as they perform a choreographed dance routine.

placed on the floor. Beside providing opportunities to have fun, camps for the hearing impaired help campers to connect with and gain the support of other young people who face similar trials.

Getting Help from the Deaf Community

Approximately five hundred thousand deaf people in the United States participate in the Deaf Community, the informal nation-wide social network of signing individuals. Because signers do not face the communication problems with each other that they face with their hearing peers, it is easy for them to feel connected. Jessica explains: "We are a close-knit community because we understand each other's pain and the limitations society erroneously tries to put on us. We know who we are and how we are more alike than different." [59]

Throughout the United States, the Deaf Community consists of groups of signing people who join together in social, athletic, and religious events. There are Deaf clubs, supported by the National Association of the Deaf. Here signers meet, visit, tell stories, and share their experiences and culture in a supportive atmosphere.

Deaf basketball leagues and bowling leagues, among other sports, are sponsored by the American Athletic Association of the Deaf. In these leagues, everyone who wants to play gets a chance to participate. To accommodate the hearing-impaired athletes and spectators, visual cues, such as flashing lights to indicate the end of a basketball quarter, are substituted for sounds. Deaf fans encourage the athletes by waving their hands instead of shouting and applauding. There are even Deaf World Games modeled after the traditional Olympics. Furthermore there are Deaf beauty contests, Deaf theater groups, and Deaf churches that conduct services in ASL.

Sharing experiences in this manner helps hearing-impaired people to develop a sense of belonging. As a result, they feel less isolated. Caring family and friends, special services and school programs, and assistive and alerting devices also provide important assistance. "Deaf and hard of hearing people can do anything they want to do," says Quishauna. "We have come a long way. And working together, we will continue to go even further." [60]

Chapter 5

What the Future Holds

Today the development of therapies to cure deafness is the focus of much research. Scientists are investigating whether gene therapy, the use of stem cells, or treatment with antioxidants can meet these goals. At the same time, many groups are promoting preventive measures to reduce the incidence of congenital and noise-induced hearing loss.

Gene Therapy

Scientists know that genetic abnormalities can cause deafness. They hope that replacing or modifying abnormal genes through a process known as gene therapy can prevent or cure deafness.

Since almost all cases of sensorineural deafness are linked to the hair cells in the inner ear, scientists are studying the genes involved in the formation and growth of these cells. They have learned that faulty genes sometimes prevent these cells from developing normally, resulting in congenital deafness. Aging, noise, and trauma also destroy the cochlear hair cells. Once compromised, the cells do not grow back. If scientists can find a gene for hair-cell regeneration, there is hope of curing deafness, or at least improving the range of hearing of many deaf individuals.

One gene that scientists are investigating, called Atoh 1, is responsible for the growth of hair cells in the inner ears of developing fetuses. Normally Atoh 1 becomes inactive after the hair cells have formed, but scientists have succeeded in reactivating it by way of genetic engineering. Inserting the modified gene into the inner ear of individuals with damaged hair cells should, scientists

In 2005 researchers performed experiments on deaf guinea pigs to prove that gene therapy can restore hearing loss in some cases.

say, stimulate enough hair-cell growth to improve or even restore an affected person's range of hearing.

In 2005 researchers at the University of Michigan–Ann Arbor tested this theory on ten profoundly deaf guinea pigs whose cochlear hair cells in both ears were destroyed with drugs. The scientists injected a virus containing the modified gene into the subjects' left inner ears, leaving the right ears to serve as controls. Since genes cannot travel through the bloodstream on their own, genetic researchers must use viruses to transmit modified genes. Subjects do not become ill because any virus used for this purpose is first rendered relatively harmless in the laboratory.

Once the animals received the gene-carrying virus, the scientists monitored their cochlear hair growth for eight weeks. At the end of this time, new hair cells were visible in the ten treated left ears. There was no new growth in the right ears.

The results proved that the procedure had stimulated new hair growth, but did not tell whether the new hair cells were functional. To determine this, the scientists administered a hearing test that measured the animals' response to sound in each of their ears. Just as the scientists predicted, all the treated ears regained some hearing, while the untreated ears did not.

Although scientists are encouraged by the results, they warn that it will take time before such a procedure can be administered to humans, mainly because the human cochlea is not as accessible as that of a guinea pig. Rather, it is located deep inside the skull, which makes inserting a virus-carrying gene difficult. Therefore, complex surgical techniques must be designed to deliver the gene to humans. Still experts are optimistic that gene therapy will be an effective treatment option for deaf individuals in the future. Commenting on the study, neuroscientist Matthew W. Kelley of the National Institute on Deafness and Other Communication Disorders, says: "The bottom line is, their hearing gets better, and that is a very big step."[61]

Replacing a Missing Protein

In 2004, while investigating the use of gene therapy to regrow cochlear hair cells, other scientists at Harvard University made an interesting discovery. They found a protein called TRPA 1 on the tip of every cochlear hair cell.

Scientists know that another TRPA protein, found in the eyes, is necessary for the conversion of light waves into electrical impulses that the brain translates into visual images. Because of its location on cochlear hair cells, the scientists think that TRPA 1 plays a similar role in hearing. If TRPA 1 is in fact needed for sound waves to be converted to electrical impulses, lack of the protein would make it impossible for sound to reach the brain.

To assess the theory, the scientists blocked the production of TRPA 1 in laboratory-cultured cochlear hair cells. Then they placed microelectrodes on the cells, exposed the cells to sound, and measured the amount of current flowing through the cells. They did the same thing to normal hair cells and compared the results. The normal cells produced electrical activity. The cells without TRPA 1 did not, validating the theory.

Because inability to produce sufficient TRPA 1 is usually inherited, scientists are currently checking blood samples from patients where deafness runs in families. If the absence of TRPA 1 is reported, scientists will start investigating ways to deliver a gene that stimulates production of the protein to affected persons' cochleas. Although accomplishing this is still in the future, scientists throughout the United States are encouraged by the study. Sunjana Chandrasekhar, an otolaryngologist at Mount Sinai School of Medicine in New York City, calls the discovery a "very meaningful step for hearing restoration."[62]

Replacing Hair Cells with Stem Cells

Other researchers are taking a different approach. They, too, are focusing on cochlear hair cells. But rather than using genes, they

An electron micrograph shows the V-shaped groups of hairs that grow from cochlear cells. Stem cells may be used to grow new hair cells.

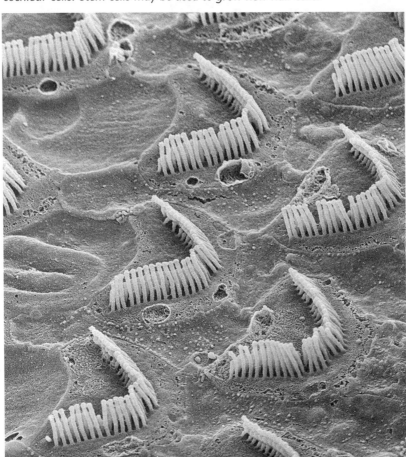

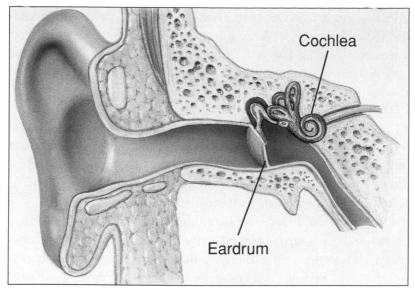

The location of the cochlea, deep in the inner ear, makes the surgical transplant of healthy cochlear hair cells a very invasive procedure.

are working on transplanting stem cells into the inner ear of subjects with sensorineural deafness.

Stem cells are unique in that they mature into any cell of any type found in the body and produce new cells of that type. Sources of stem cells include human embryos created in fertilization clinics, aborted fetuses, and the bone marrow of adults and children. Once the cells have been harvested, they are taken to a laboratory where scientists have developed a method to make the cells multiply and survive indefinitely.

Researchers theorize that healthy stem cells can be transplanted into the inner ear of individuals with damaged cochlear hair cells. The transplanted cells, they believe, will quickly take on the characteristics and function of healthy cochlear hair cells, essentially curing sensorineural deafness.

Once again, however, the inaccessibility of the cochlea makes application of the proposed treatment problematic. Since directly inserting stem cells into the human cochlea is so difficult, scientists are working on transforming these stem cells into cochlear hair cells in a laboratory. This way, instead of subjecting a patient to the invasive surgery necessary to deliver cells to the cochlea, the transformed cells can be inserted into the outer ear. Since transformed stem cells seek out like cells, the scientists speculate that the therapeutic cells will naturally find their way to the inner ear.

Progress in Stem-Cell Research

By 2003 Harvard University scientists working at the Massachusetts Eye and Ear Infirmary in Boston managed to grow inner-ear hair cells from cultured embryonic mouse stem cells. To do this, the researchers treated the stem cells with chemicals and a growth factor similar to natural substances found in the inner ear. To see if the lab-grown cells could survive and function inside a living creature, the scientists implanted the cells into embryonic chickens. This was done by making a small hole in the egg and injecting the cells. Because chicken embryos have no immune system, the embryos did not reject the mouse cells. As the scientists hoped, the implanted cells quickly found their way to the developing chickens' inner ears and gave rise to cochlear hair cells.

Based on the results of this study, scientists are working on creating cochlear hair cells using human stem cells. It will be at least ten years before stem-cell therapy is likely to offer a viable way to treat deafness. But the Harvard study has made many experts and deaf people hopeful. Indeed, according to authors Karen Watters and Eduardo C. Corrales in an article in *ENT: Ear, Nose, & Throat Journal,* "It is exciting to speculate on the impact these findings will have on the future of clinical treatment of inner ear disorders. At the moment, it seems futuristic to envision therapy with progenitor cell grafts [stem cells]. . . . But it is conceivable that these dreams will eventually be realized."[63]

Use of Vitamins to Restore Hearing

Israeli scientists are taking a completely different approach to restoring hearing. Instead of trying to replace damaged cochlear hair cells, they are investigating the biological event that causes the damage and considering how to counteract it. Scientists know that when experimental animals are suddenly deafened by noise, drugs, or disease, a process called oxidation occurs in the animals' cochleas.

Treating Noise-Induced Deafness with Gene Therapy

A 2005 study conducted jointly at Harvard University and Massachusetts General Hospital in Boston looked at Rb 1, a gene that acts as an off switch, deactivating fetal cochlear hair-cell growth once adequate cells have formed. Modifying or removing Rb 1, scientists hypothesize, eliminates any controls on cochlear hair-cell growth, making it possible for damaged cells to regenerate on an ongoing basis. If the theory is correct, modifying or removing Rb 1 could be especially effective in treating individuals, such as musicians or miners, whose hearing has been damaged by continued exposure to loud noise.

To test the theory, the scientists bred a strain of mice lacking the Rb 1 gene and monitored the inner ears of the offspring from birth until death. The mice were born with more cochlear hair than normal, and the growth did not stop as the animals aged.

As more cochlear hair formed, however, the mice exhibited problems with balance. As a result, the scientists say that uncontrollable inner-ear growth leads to balance disorders. Therefore, although treating noise-induced deafness with Rb 1 has potential, similar tests cannot be done on humans until scientists have found a way to deactivate the hair-growth process.

Scientists are now working on ways to solve this problem. When this is accomplished, treatment with the gene may not be far behind. In an article titled "Gene That Blocks Regrowth of Hearing Cells Identified for the First Time" on the National Institute on Deafness and Other Communication Disorders Web site, director James Battey explains that this discovery is "a very important first step towards learning how to restore hearing in human patients."

That is, oxygen molecules known as free radicals begin to damage or destroy healthy cells. In the ears, the victims are hair cells.

Using this knowledge as a basis for their theory, in 2003 researchers at Rambam Medical Center and the Technion-Israel Institute of Technology in Haifa decided to treat suddenly deafened individuals with large doses of an antioxidant, a substance that destroys free radicals and thus combats the effects of oxidation. They hoped that the antioxidants would lessen the effect of free radicals and have a restorative role in the inner ear.

The scientists tested the effects of vitamin E, well known for its antioxidant properties, on a group of sixty-six suddenly deafened adults. Usually suddenly deafened persons are treated with steroid injections, which results in the recovery of some, but not all, patients. In this study half the subjects were administered steroids plus four hundred milligrams of vitamin E twice a day, while the control population received steroids only.

To determine the effectiveness of the vitamin, the subjects' recovery rate, which was a measurement of the improvement in their range of hearing, was tracked. The scientists found that 78 percent of the vitamin E group showed marked improvement in their range of hearing, compared to 45 percent of the control group.

Use of Other Antioxidants to Restore Hearing

Based on the results of the Israeli study, in 2003 scientists from the U.S. Naval Medical Center in San Diego, California; the American BioHealth Group, a San Diego pharmaceutical company; and the University of Buffalo's Center for Hearing and Deafness in New York conducted a joint study on 550 U.S. Marines during two weeks of war games. During that time, the marines were exposed to high levels of noise from gunfire and explosions that could cause noise-induced hearing loss.

The aim of the study was to find out whether treatment with antioxidants could not only restore hearing but also prevent noise-induced hearing loss from occurring. To find out, the scientists gave half of the marines an eight-ounce glass full of an antioxidant compound known as *N*-acetylcystine, NAC, with every meal. The other group received a placebo, that is, a medically in-

The sounds of gunfire and explosions can deafen soldiers. Recent research, however, has shown that antioxidants can help prevent noise-induced hearing loss.

active substance such as a sugar pill. Both groups were administered hearing tests before the study began, when it ended, and six months afterward. The hearing tests showed that the group that was administered NAC experienced 40 percent less permanent hearing loss than the placebo group. Based on these findings, preventive treatment with antioxidant supplements will likely become a way to protect the hearing of people exposed to ongoing noise in the future.

Consumers can now buy a pill similar to that used in the 2003 study, known as the "hearing pill," from the American BioHealth group. Because the pill is an antioxidant and is being marketed as a dietary supplement, it does not need federal government approval.

Before similar pills can be marketed as preventive medical treatment for hearing loss, more studies must be conducted. If the results of the new studies are comparable to the 2003 study, scientists predict that antioxidant compounds will be approved by the FDA as a hearing-loss preventive treatment by 2007. Executives of American BioHealth believe that the hearing pill will be the first of a number of safe and effective products for hearing loss and related conditions.

Taking Preventive Measures

Advocacy groups made up of scientists, activists, educators, civic leaders, environmentalists, health-care professionals, and concerned citizens are trying to prevent noise-induced hearing loss in another way. They are working to raise public awareness of the dangers of loud noise, as well as taking steps to control it.

Groups such as Noise Free America, Noise Off, and the League for the Hard of Hearing, to name just a few, are dedicated to fighting excess noise, which is also known as noise pollution. With chapters throughout the world, these groups work to protect the public from noise pollution in a number of ways.

One way is by testing the noise level of popular toys and publishing the results. Many toys are noisy enough to be harmful to children. Most adults are unaware of which toys are most likely to put youngsters at risk.

 # Scientists Develop a Mechanical Cochlea

In 2005 scientists at the University of Michigan–Ann Arbor developed the first artificial cochlea. Someday the device may be used to take over the job of the cochleas of individuals with sensorineural hearing loss.

Only very slightly larger than the natural organ, the artificial cochlea is a micro-machine built in size and shape to exactly match the human cochlea. Help for Hearing Loss, a Web site dedicated to providing news and information about hearing loss, describes the invention:

> The mechanical cochlea works in the same way as its biological counterpart. In the biological cochlea, the basilar membrane, which winds along the cochlear spiral, is stiffer at the base and becomes softer as it approaches the center. In the engineered cochlea . . . a fluid-filled duct etched onto a chip acts as the cochlear spiral. When sound waves enter the

According to the federal government, exposure to noise levels of ninety decibels and above can cause permanent hearing damage in a relatively short time, and many toys exceed this level. At the urging of groups opposed to noise pollution, the American Society for Testing and Materials, a developer of standards in 130 technical fields, published a 2004 acoustic standard regarding the loudness of toys, stating that toys should not exceed ninety decibels. However, compliance is voluntary and many toys exceed this level. Even those that do not can pose a risk for young children whose shorter arm span results in their holding toys closer to their ears, which amplifies the sound. Indeed, a rattle held close to the ear can easily produce 94 dB. By testing popular toys and publishing the results, these organizations give concerned adults the tools to make informed decisions about what toys are safest for their children.

mechanical cochlea's input membrane, a wave is created, which travels down the duct, interacting with a tapered micro-machined membrane, analogous to the basilar membrane. This process allows the device to separate different frequency tones.

The device is still in its early stages of development, years from being used to replace a damaged cochlea. But researchers are optimistic that it can be used in the near future in conjunction with a cochlear implant to improve implantees' hearing and perhaps eliminate the need for external equipment. The article explains:

The goal is to use the mechanical cochlea as a sensitive microphone . . . the same way an external microphone, a microprocessor, and an antenna work together in present implants. Cochlear implants work by sending signals for different frequencies to electrodes implanted in the cochlear spiral. . . . Researchers are adding arrays of sensors to the mechanical cochlea, which would make it possible to use the new device to drive the electrodes in a cochlear implant.

Many video games and other popular toys produce enough noise to cause permanent hearing damage in a very short time.

In addition to letting consumers know which toys are safest, these groups organize boycotts of toy manufacturers that consistently produce loud toys. They also promote boycotts of stores and manufacturers that produce other dangerously loud items such as leaf blowers, hot rod mufflers, automobile stereo systems, and car alarms. The organizations say that if enough financial pressure is exerted on businesses involved in the production and sale of such items, the businesses will modify or stop selling the offending products.

Controlling Noise in Schools

Protecting children from noise-induced hearing loss is also the focus of a program known as Quiet Classrooms, sponsored by an alliance of nonprofit organizations such as the Acoustical Society of America and the Noise Pollution Clearinghouse. Working together, educators, students, parents, and architects are creating designs for new schools with noise reduction in mind, as well as making changes in existing schools. For example, Quiet Classrooms is doing whatever it takes to ensure that new schools are located away from highways, railroad crossings, and airplane flight paths that produce high noise levels. When this is not possible, they are urging new and existing schools to install double-paned windows to help reduce outside sound, as well as adding carpeting and insulated ceiling tiles that absorb excess noise. They are also helping schools to make minor changes that can go a long way in protecting students' ears. Such changes range from having maintenance people mow lawns, blow leaves, and make repairs after school hours, to moving students' desks away from loud wall-mounted air conditioners and heating pumps.

School cafeterias are another target. According to Quiet Classrooms, school cafeterias tend to have few surfaces that absorb sound. Noise from normal conversations, clattering trays and silverware, and scraping chairs becomes amplified as it bounces off bare

Crowded, enclosed areas, including school cafeterias, often have dangerously high noise levels.

walls, ceilings, and floors. As a result, people often must shout just to be heard. The effect is like adding the voices of several hundred additional people to the room. It is not surprising, then, that noise in school cafeterias commonly exceeds 90 dB. According to Dina, an educator, "My school cafeteria is so noisy, it makes my ears ring when I go in there. There are so many kids, and they seem so loud because the sound echoes so much. You can't hear anything. Everyone shouts. I think it has to do with the way they built it. There is no insulation. The acoustics are terrible."[64]

Some schools are trying to improve cafeteria acoustics by adding foam paneling to the walls and ceilings. Other schools are experimenting with a stoplight that measures decibel levels in their cafeterias. Mounted to the cafeteria wall where it is clearly visible, the stoplight works like a traffic signal. A green light indicates sound levels are safe. A yellow light warns that sound levels are nearing dangerous levels. A red light alerts students and faculty that sound levels exceed 90 dB. Such a system helps students and faculty to monitor noise levels and reduce the volume whenever levels become dangerous.

Educating the Public

Children and schools are also the focus of other programs such as Stop That Noise!, the Dangerous Decibels Project, and Wise Ears. These programs are sponsored by nonprofit organizations, concerned businesses, state and local governments, and school districts. The first two programs aim to educate young people to the dangers of noise. They provide hands-on, multimedia educational material to schools in an effort to change students' attitude and behavior when it comes to loud noise. For example, a typical lesson alerts students to the danger of listening to loud music through personal stereo systems and then allows students to experience noise-induced hearing loss through a simulation using an audio cassette.

Wise Ears has even a wider focus. This national campaign sponsored by the National Institute on Deafness and Other Communication Disorders seeks to educate not just children but also adults by means of school programs, printed and electronic material, radio announcements, and public meetings. Wise Ears is aimed at raising public awareness about noise-induced hearing loss and providing the public with the tools to protect their hearing. This includes providing workers in high-noise professions with ear plugs that lessen the impact of loud noise. The goal of Wise Ears is to

> increase awareness about noise-induced hearing loss (NIHL) among all audiences. . . . Motivate all audiences to take action against NIHL by understanding the problem and its solutions, e.g., understanding that everyone is at risk for NIHL; expanding the availability of hearing protection devices; advocating changes in the workplace; developing hearing loss prevention programs. [65]

Passing Laws

Another way advocacy groups are working to prevent noise-induced hearing loss is by working with elected officials to enact laws against noise pollution. Currently, many state and local governments have set standards and passed laws controlling noise. Some laws are limited to noise at construction sites, airports, car-racing facilities, and firing ranges. Other laws set limits on noise produced by motorcycles, snow mobiles, burglar alarms, and car stereos. In some states, like California, Delaware, and New Jersey, for example, the laws limit all types of noise pollution. But there is no comprehensive federal law against noise pollution. Activists hope to change this. Representatives such as New York congresswoman Nita Lowey agree. Lowey, who is sponsoring a law that would limit noise nationwide, calls noise pollution "truly a public health threat," and stresses the need to "work to diminish the impact noise has on our communities." [66]

Preventing Congenital Deafness

Other groups such as the March of Dimes and state health-care agencies are taking different preventive measures. They are working to prevent congenital deafness by making women aware of the steps in ensuring a healthy pregnancy. For example, they urge all women to have a thorough checkup before becoming pregnant. A physical examination including routine lab work is a good

With the help of a physician, this pregnant woman hopes to minimize the risk of giving birth to a baby with congenital problems, including deafness.

way to evaluate a woman's overall health. In addition, it gives the woman an opportunity to bring all vaccinations up-to-date, a measure that protects babies from the rubella virus, which causes deafness in the fetus. At the same time, the woman is screened and treated for sexually transmitted diseases, which can also damage developing cochlear cells and cause congenital deafness.

Women are also given information about the harmful effects of medications, illegal drugs, dangerous chemicals, and alcohol. Armed with this information, women can protect their babies by avoiding these substances during pregnancy. They are also educated about the importance of adequate prenatal care and good nutrition during pregnancy. These are two essential ways to help prevent premature births, which often lead to congenital deafness. According to the Texas Medical Association, "Taking care of your body before, as well as during, pregnancy provides the best prevention of future health problems in your baby."[67]

With so many groups working to prevent new cases of deafness from occurring, and scientists developing ways to cure or lessen the effects of hearing loss, the future looks bright. One day soon, deafness may be a condition of the past.

Notes

Introduction: Lack of Knowledge Leads to Problems

1. Elizabeth Tricase, "Treat Us Fairly," *World Around You,* Spring/Summer 2002, p. 12. www.clerccenter.gallaudet.edu/World AroundYou/Spr-Sum-2002/commendable2.pdf.
2. Quoted in Kathryn P. Meadows-Orlans, Donna M. Mertens, and Marilyn A. Sass-Lehrer, *Parents and Their Deaf Children.* Washington, DC: Gallaudet University Press, 2003, p. 149.
3. NFD, "Deafness—The Invisible Handicap," September 2002. www.nfd.org.nz/nfdnews/mediareleases/deafnessthein visiblehandicap.
4. Jessica Ann Kellerman, "Our Stars and Ourselves," *World Around You,* Spring/Summer 2002, p. 8. www.clerccenter. gallaudet.edu/WorldAroundYou/Spr-Sum-2002/kellerman.pdf.

Chapter 1: What Is Deafness?

5. Interview with the author in Las Cruces, New Mexico, January 25, 2005.
6. Quoted in Cynthia Farley, *Bridge to Sound with a 'Bionic' Ear.* Wayzata, MN: Periscope, 2002, p. 347.
7. Quoted in Meadows-Orlans et al., *Parents and Their Deaf Children,* p. 81.
8. Beverly Biderman, *Wired for Sound.* Toronto: Trifolium, 1998, p. 42.
9. Quoted in Farley, *Bridge to Sound with a 'Bionic' Ear,* p. 146.
10. Quoted in Farley, *Bridge to Sound with a 'Bionic' Ear,* p. 91.
11. Stephanie Foote, "An Exciting Life," *World Around You,* Fall 2002, p. 14. www.clerccenter.gallaudet.edu/WorldAround You/Fall-2002/foote.pdf.

12. Quoted in Shannon Mullen, "Now Hear This! Life Is Getting Louder," *Las Cruces Sun News,* December 26, 2003, p. 6C.

13. Quoted in Jeffrey Kluger, "Just Too Loud," *Time,* April 5, 2004, p. 55.

14. Quoted in Farley, *Bridge to Sound with a 'Bionic' Ear,* p. 355.

15. Michelle Koplitz, "My Sister," *World Around You,* Summer 2003, p. 8. www.clerccenter.gallaudet.edu/WorldAroundYou/Summer2003/HonMention1.pdf.

16. Biderman, *Wired for Sound,* p. 48.

17. Quoted in Farley, *Bridge to Sound with a 'Bionic' Ear,* p. 379.

18. Quoted in Nanci A. Scheetz, *Orientation to Deafness.* Boston: Allyn and Bacon, 2001, p. 104.

19. Matthew S. Moore and Linda Levitan, *For Hearing People Only.* Rochester, NY: Deaf Life, 1993, p. 133.

Chapter 2: Diagnosis and Treatment

20. Interview with the author in Las Cruces, New Mexico, March 3, 2005.

21. Quoted in Farley, *Bridge to Sound with a 'Bionic' Ear,* p. 142.

22. Interview with the author in Las Cruces, New Mexico, January 25, 2005.

23. Harriet Rose, "Growing Accustomed," *Chevy Chaser Magazine.* www.chevychaser.com/rose.html.

24. Healthy Hearing, "A New Twist in Sound Clarity." www.healthyhearing.com/library/testimonial_content.asp?testimonial_id=170.

25. Healthy Hearing, "A New Twist in Sound Clarity."

26. Healthy Hearing, "Floyd (Dad) and Nichole (10 Years Old)." www.healthyhearing.com/library/testimonial_content.asp?testimonial_id=176.

27. John M. Burkey, *Overcoming Hearing Aid Fears.* New Brunswick, NJ: Rutgers University Press, 2003, p. 74.

28. Interview with the author in Las Cruces, New Mexico, March 3, 2005.

29. Healthy Hearing, "A New Twist in Sound Clarity."

30. Jan Pudlow, "After 40 Years Lawyer Regains Hearing," Hearing Exchange. www.hearingexchange.com/articles/a-archives.

31. Quoted in *People,* "A Joyful Noise," October 2, 2002, p. 87.

32. Quoted in Pudlow, "After 40 Years Lawyer Regains Hearing."
33. Kellerman, "Our Stars and Ourselves," p. 8.

Chapter 3: Many Ways to Communicate
34. Quoted in Meadows-Orlans et al., *Parents and Their Deaf Children*, p. 20.
35. Hearing Exchange, "Hear Our Parents." www.hearing exchange.com/hear_our_parents.htm.
36. Laurie Monsebraate, "Annie's Miracle—Part II," Learning to Listen Foundation. www.learningtolisten.org/stories.htm.
37. Julie Burnham-Ward, "Can You Hear the Crickets Sing?" Learning to Listen Foundation. www.learningtolisten.org/stories.htm.
38. Quoted in Biderman, *Wired for Sound*, p. 57.
39. Henry Kisor, *What's That Pig Outdoors?* New York: Hill & Wang, 1990, p. 36.
40. Quoted in Meadows-Orlans et al., *Parents and Their Deaf Children*, p. 90.
41. Quoted in Meadows-Orlans et al., *Parents and Their Deaf Children*, p. 24.
42. Quoted in Biderman, *Wired for Sound*, p. 116.
43. Interview with the author in Las Cruces, New Mexico, January 8, 2005.
44. Kisor, *What's That Pig Outdoors?*, p. 75.
45. Kisor, *What's That Pig Outdoors?*, p. 103.
46. Quoted in Meadows-Orlans et al., *Parents and Their Deaf Children*, p. 19.

Chapter 4: Living with Deafness
47. Jonathan Lai, "Sympathy? Special Treatment? No Thanks!" *World Around You,* Spring/Summer 2002, p. 4. www.clerccenter.gallaudet.edu/WorldAroundYou/Spr-Sum-2002/first.pdf.
48. Quoted in Farley, *Bridge to Sound with a 'Bionic' Ear*, p. 219.
49. Quishauna Harrison, "We've Come a Long Way," *World Around You*, Spring/Summer 2002, p. 11. www.clerccenter.gallaudet.edu/WorldAroundYou/Spr-Sum-2002/commendable1.pdf.
50. Stephanie Foote, "View from the Seventh Grade, My Life with Hearing Loss," *Odyssey*, Winter 2003, p. 28. www.clerccenter.gallaudet.edu/odyssey/Winter2003/seventhgrade.pdf.

51. Biderman, *Wired for Sound,* p. 44.
52. Quoted in Abigail Van Buren, "Detecting Early Hearing Loss Gives Kids Lifelong Benefits," *Las Cruces Sun News,* February 18, 2005, p. 4C.
53. Interview with the author in Las Cruces, New Mexico, March 3, 2005.
54. Claire Bugen, "Overview," Texas School for the Deaf. www.tsd.state.tx.us/overview/index.htm.
55. Bugen, "Overview."
56. Kellerman, "Our Stars and Ourselves," p. 8.
57. Quoted in Farley, *Bridge to Sound with a 'Bionic' Ear,* p. 254.
58. Quoted in Farley, *Bridge to Sound with a 'Bionic' Ear,* p. 354.
59. Jessica Fletcher, "More Alike than Different," *World Around You,* Spring/Summer 2002, p. 7. www.clerccenter.gallaudet.edu/WorldAroundYou/Spr-Sum-2002/third.pdf.
60. Harrison, "We've Come a Long Way," p. 11.

Chapter 5: What the Future Holds
61. Quoted in Thomas H. Maugh II, "Deaf Animals Regain Hearing," North Jersey.com, February 14, 2005. www.bergen.com/page.php?qstr=eXJpcnk3ZjczN2Y3dnFlZUVFeXk2MTEmZmdiZ.
62. Quoted in *Palm Beach Daily News,* "Scientists Find Molecular Key to Hearing," October, 13, 2004. www.palmbeachdailynews.com/health/content/shared-auto/healthnews/deaf/521749.html.
63. Karen Watters and Eduardo C. Corrales, "Feasibility of Treating Hearing Disorders with Stem Cells," *ENT: Ear, Nose & Throat Journal,* October 2004, p. 689.
64. Interview with the author in Las Cruces, New Mexico, April 3, 2005.
65. NIDCD, "Wise Ears!" www.nidcd.nih.gov/health/wise/index.asp.
66. Quoted in J. Kluger, "Just Too Loud," p. 55.
67. Michael L. Schultz, "Getting Ready for a Healthy Pregnancy," *Homepage for Dr. Michael L. Schultz.* www.mlschultz.yourmd.com.

Glossary

alerting device: A device that alerts people with hearing loss to important events without the use of sound.

American Sign Language (ASL): The visible language used in the United States by many deaf people.

assistive device: Any tool that makes life easier for a disabled person.

audiologist: A healthcare professional who is trained to evaluate and treat hearing loss.

auditory nerve: The nerve that carries electrical impulses from the inner ear to the brain.

auditory-verbal therapy: A form of therapy that teaches deaf people to become more aware of sound in order to develop oral language.

closed captioning: A system that translates the audio segment of a television program into text that scrolls along the bottom of the screen.

cochlea: A snail-like structure in the inner ear where sound waves are converted to electrical impulses.

cochlear implant: A medical device implanted in the cochlea that improves hearing.

conductive deafness: Deafness caused by problems in the outer or middle ear.

congenital deafness: Deafness that occurs before or during birth.

cued speech: A visual communication system that uses eight hand shapes and four hand positions near the mouth to distinguish between sounds that look alike on the lips.

Deaf Community: The term used to describe signing people.

deafness: The decreased ability to hear sound.

decidel (dB): A unit used to measure the volume of sound.

eardrum (tympanic membrane): A thin membrane that separates the outer and middle ear. It vibrates when sound waves hit it.

finger spelling: A type of visual language that uses the fingers to represent the letters of the alphabet. It is often combined with sign language.

frequency: The number of vibrations per second a sound wave produces, which determines the sound's pitch.

frequency modulation (FM) system: An assistive device that uses radio waves to make sound more accessible to people with hearing loss when they are in a classroom or large lecture hall.

gene therapy: A process in which defective genes are modified or replaced with healthy genes.

hertz (Hz): A unit used to measure the frequency of sound.

laryngograph: A device that measures the pitch, breathiness, and intensity of a person's speech.

ossicles: Three tiny bones in the middle ear whose movement sends sound to the inner ear.

otologist: A doctor who specializes in treating the ear.

otosclerosis: A condition in which spongy tissue grows over the ossicles, making it difficult for them to move.

otoscope: A device used to visually exam the ear.

oval window: The entrance to the inner ear.

postlingual deafness: Deafness that occurs after language is acquired.

prelingual deafness: Deafness that occurs before language is acquired.

relay service: A telephone service in which a human operator reads a TTY message to a hearing recipient and transcribes an oral message into text for a deaf caller.

sensorineural deafness: Deafness caused by problems in the inner ear.

sign language: A visible language that uses the hands, fingers, facial muscles, and body language to communicate ideas.

sound wave: Vibrations in the air caused when an object is struck by an outside force.

speechreading (lipreading): A way to discern spoken language by focusing intently on the movement of a speaker's lips, mouth, tongue, and jaws, and linking these movements to the sounds and words that they ordinarily form.

speech therapy: A form of therapy that helps people to speak more clearly.

stapedectomy: Surgery in which damaged ossicles are replaced by artificial bone.

Total Communication: A communication system that combines oral speech, sign language, and speechreading.

TTY: A telecommunications system that allows users to send and receive text messages through regular phone lines.

tympanoplasty: Surgery that repairs a torn eardrum.

video relay service (VRS): A telephone system that allows signers to communicate with hearing people via a Web camera connected to the Internet.

Organizations to Contact

Alexander Graham Bell Association for the Deaf and Hard of Hearing
3417 Volta Place, NW Washington, DC 20007
tollfree: (866) 337-5220 (Voice)
(202) 337-5221 (TTY)
Web site: www.agbell.org

This organization promotes the use of oral language as the primary communication method for the deaf. It offers information on cochlear implants, auditory-verbal and speech therapy, assistive devices, and schools and camps for the deaf. It publishes a number of magazines, and has a special section for teens with hearing loss.

Gallaudet University
800 Florida Ave. NE Washington, DC 20002
(202) 651-5050 (TTY)
Web site: www.gallaudet.edu

Gallaudet University is the only university in the world for the deaf. In addition to providing hearing-impaired individuals with an education, it offers information about the university to the public. It also has a career center and a large library. It is the home to the Laurent Clerc Deaf Education Center, which provides all sorts of information on deafness to the public.

League of the Hard of Hearing
71 West 23rd St. New York, NY 10010-4162
(917) 305-7700 (Voice)

(917) 305-7999 (TTY)

Web site: www.lhh.org

Provides information and support for people with hearing loss. It also sponsors Stop That Noise!, an education program aimed at preventing noise-induced hearing loss.

March of Dimes

1275 Mamaroneck Ave. White Plains, NY 10605

(914) 428-7100 (Voice)

Web site: www.modimes.org

One of the largest organizations working to end birth defects, including congenital deafness. With chapters throughout the United States, it provides information on pregnancy issues and birth defects.

National Association of the Deaf

814 Thayer Ave. Silver Spring, MD 20910-4500

(301) 587-1788 (Voice)

(301) 587-1789 (TTY)

Web site: www.nad.org

Part of the World Association of the Deaf, this organization provides information to the public on deafness. It works to protect the rights of deaf people and advocates for research and laws.

National Institute on Deafness and Other Communication Disorders (NIDCD)

31 Center Drive, MSC 2320 Bethesda, MD 20892-2320

(301) 496-7243 (Voice)

(301) 402-0252 (TTY)

e-mail: nidcdinfo@nidcd.nih.gov

Web site: www.nidcd.nih.gov/index.asp

Part of the National Institutes of Health, NIDCD provides information on deafness, sponsors research, and works to raise public awareness about hearing loss.

Noise Free America

PO Box 2202 Indianapolis, IN 46206

(765) 658-4493 (Voice)

Web site: www.noisefree.org

With chapters throughout the United States, this group speaks to community groups, testifies before city councils, and hosts meetings in an effort to fight noise pollution. Their Internet site provides information and noise-complaint cards that citizens can send to stores that sell noisy products.

Self Help for Hard of Hearing People (SHHH)
7910 Woodmount Ave. Suite 1200 Bethesda, MD 20814
(301) 657-2248 (Voice)
(301) 657-2249 (TTY)
Web site: www.shhh.org

This organization sponsors local chapters throughout the United States. It organizes support groups, provides information on assistive devices, cochlear implants, and hearing aids. It also publishes a magazine called the *Hearing Loss Journal*.

For Further Reading

Books

Carol Baldwin, *Hearing Loss.* Chicago: Heinemann Library, 2002. A young-adult book that discusses the causes and types of hearing loss and the effects it has on people's lives.

Carol Basinger, *Everything You Need to Know About Deafness.* New York: Rosen, 2000. A simple book that looks at the workings of the ear, causes of deafness, and prevention.

Jackie Kramer, *You Can Learn Sign Language: More than 300 Words in Pictures.* New York: Troll Books, 2000. A simple illustrated introduction to sign language.

Carol Padden and Tom Humphries, *Deaf in America: Voices From a Culture.* Boston: Harvard University Press, 2000. Looks at deaf culture, deaf arts and theater, signing, and the controversies surrounding the deaf.

Adan R. Penilla and Angela Lee Taylor, *Signing for Dummies.* Foster City, CA: IDG Books Worldwide, 2003. Teaches sign language in a simple, sequential manner. A DVD is included with the book to help illustrate the signs.

Web Sites

Deaf Today (www.deaftoday.com). Offers current news from around the world pertaining to deafness, people with hearing loss, and the Deaf Community, as well as an archive.

Hearing Education and Awareness for Rockers (www.hear net.com/index.shtml). This group works to raise musicians' awareness of noise-induced hearing loss by providing information and solutions.

Hearing Exchange (www.hearingexchange.com). An online community that offers information and support for hearing-impaired people and their loved ones. Includes message boards, jokes, and solutions to some of the challenges hearing-impaired people face.

Help for Hearing Loss (www.hearinglossweb.com). Provides information and support for hard-of-hearing people, including news on the latest research, discussion of social and legal issues, and medical information.

Laurent Clerc National Deafness Education Center (www.clerc center.gallaudet.edu). A part of Gallaudet University, the center offers a wealth of information about every aspect of deafness. It also provides a lending library and publishes two magazines, *World Around You* and *Odyssey*. Both publications are for teens and are available on the Web site.

Learning to Listen Foundation (www.learningtolisten.org). Offers information about auditory-verbal therapy.

Quiet Classrooms (www.quietclassrooms.org). This organization works to reduce noise in schools. It offers information and solutions, including steps students can take.

Works Consulted

Books

Beverly Biderman, *Wired for Sound*. Toronto: Trifolium, 1998. One of the first patients to receive a cochlear implant, the profoundly deaf author talks about her life, the challenges she faced, why she chose to receive an implant, and the controversy concerning cochlear implants.

John M. Burkey, *Overcoming Hearing Aid Fears*. New Brunswick, NJ: Rutgers University Press, 2003. Talks about the different types of hearing aids and how they work.

Cynthia Farley, *Bridge to Sound with a 'Bionic' Ear*. Wayzata, MN: Periscope, 2002. Adults, teens, and children discuss their hearing loss, their lives, and their experiences with hearing aids and cochlear implants.

Henry Kisor, *What's That Pig Outdoors?* New York: Hill & Wang, 1990. A humorous and inspiring autobiography by a profoundly deaf writer, journalist, and newspaper editor. Kisor talks about his life, the challenges he faced, and how he succeeded.

Kathryn P. Meadows-Orlans, Donna M. Mertens, and Marilyn A. Sass-Lehrer, *Parents and Their Deaf Children*. Washington, DC: Gallaudet University Press, 2003. Details the experiences of parents of deaf children.

Matthew S. Moore and Linda Levitan, *For Hearing People Only*. Rochester, NY: Deaf Life, 1993. The profoundly deaf authors are prominent members of the Deaf Community. In an easy-to-read manner, the book dispels popular misconceptions about deafness.

Nanci A. Scheetz, *Orientation to Deafness*. Boston: Allyn and Bacon, 2001. A college textbook that looks at deafness and the education of deaf children.

Carol Turkington and Allen E. Sussman, *The Encyclopedia of Deafness and Hearing Disorders*. New York: Facts On File, 2000. From A to Z, this book discusses every aspect of deafness including famous deaf people.

Periodicals
Jeffrey Kluger, "Just Too Loud," *Time*, April 5, 2004.

Shannon Mullen, "Now Hear This! Life Is Getting Louder," *Las Cruces Sun News*, December 26, 2003.

People, "A Joyful Noise," October 2, 2002.

Abigail Van Buren, "Detecting Early Hearing Loss Gives Kids Lifelong Benefits," *Las Cruces Sun News*, February 18, 2005.

Karen Watters and Eduardo C. Corrales, "Feasibility of Treating Hearing Disorders with Stem Cells," *ENT: Ear, Nose & Throat Journal*, October 2004.

Internet Sources
Claire Bugen, "Overview," Texas School for the Deaf. www.tsd.state.tx.us/overview/index.htm.

Julie Burnham-Ward, "Can You Hear the Crickets Sing?" Learning to Listen Foundation. www.learningtolisten.org/stories.htm.

Warren Estabrooks, "Lesson Plans," Learning to Listen Foundation. www.learningto listen.org/stories.

———, "What is Auditory-Verbal Therapy (AVT)?" Learning to Listen Foundation. www.learningtolisten.org/faq1_whats_avt.html.

Jessica Fletcher, "More Alike than Different," *World Around You*, Spring/Summer 2002. www.clerccenter.gallaudet.edu/World AroundYou/Spr-Sum-2002/third.pdf.

Stephanie Foote, "An Exciting Life," *World Around You*, Fall 2002. www. clerccenter.gallaudet.edu/World AroundYou/Fall-2002/foote.pdf.

———, "View from the Seventh Grade, My Life with Hearing Loss," *Odyssey*, Winter 2003. www.clerccenter.gallaudet.edu/odyssey/Winter2003/seventhgrade.pdf.

Quishauna Harrison, "We've Come a Long Way," *World Around You*, Spring/Summer 2002. www.clerccenter.gallaudet.edu/World AroundYou/Spr-Sum-2002/commendable1.pdf.

Healthy Hearing, "Floyd (Dad) and Nichole (10 years Old)." www.healthyhearing.com/library/testimonialcontent.asp?test imonial_id=176.

———, "A New Twist in Sound Clarity." www.healthyhearing.com/library/testimonialcontent.asp?testimonial_id=170.

Hearing Dogs for Deaf People, "Our Recipients." www.hearing-dogs.co.uk/our-recipients.html.

Hearing Exchange, "Hear Our Parents." www.hearingexchange.com/hear_our_parents.htm.

The Hearing Pill, "American BioHealth Group Announces Availability of the Hearing Pill." www.thehearingpill.com/index.asp?PageAction=Custom&ID=16.

Help for Hearing Loss, "Hearing Loss Cures." www.hearingloss web.com/Medical/cures/cures.htm.

Jessica Ann Kellerman, "Our Stars and Ourselves," *World Around You,* Spring/Summer 2002. www.clerccenter.gallaudet.edu/WorldAroundYou/Spr-Sum-2002/kellerman.pdf.

Michelle Koplitz, "My Sister," *World Around You,* Summer 2003. www.clerccenter.gallaudet.edu/WorldAroundYou/Summer 2003/HonMention1.pdf.

Jonathan Lai, "Sympathy? Special Treatment? No Thanks!" *World Around You,* Spring/Summer 2002. www.clerccenter.gallaudet.edu/WorldAroundYou/Spr-Sum-2002/first.pdf.

Thomas H. Maugh II, "Deaf Animals Regain Hearing," North Jersey.com. www.bergen.com/page.php?qstr=eXJpcnk3Zjcz N2Y3dnFlZUVFeXk2MTEmZmdiZ.

Laurie Monsebraate, "Annie's Miracle—Part II," Learning to Listen Foundation. www.learningtolisten.org/stories.htm.

NFD, "Deafness—The Invisible Handicap," September 2002. www.nfd.org.nz/nfdnews/mediareleases/deafnesstheinvisible handicap.

NIDCD, "Gene That Blocks Regrowth of Hearing Cells Identified for the First Time." www.nidcd.nih.gov/news/releases/05/1_19_05.asp.

———, "Wise Ears!" www.nidcd.nih.gov/health/wise/index.asp.

Palm Beach Daily News, "Scientists Find Molecular Key to Hearing," October 13, 2004. www.palmbeachdailynews.com/health/content/shared-auto/healthnews/deaf/521749.html.

Jan Pudlow, "After 40 Years Lawyer Regains Hearing," Hearing Exchange. www.hearingexchange.com/stories.htm.

Quiet Classrooms, "What Noise Sources Cause Most Problems?" www.quietclassrooms.org/library/problems.htm.

Harriet Rose, "Growing Accustomed," *Chevy Chaser Magazine*. www.chevychaser.com/rose.html.

Michael L. Schultz, "Getting Ready for a Healthy Pregnancy," *Homepage of Dr. Michael L. Schultz*. www.mlschultz.yourmd.com.

Elizabeth Tricase, "Treat Us Fairly," *World Around You*, Spring/Summer 2002. www.clerccenter.gallaudet.edu/WorldAround You/Spr-Sum-2002/commendable2.pdf.

Index

Acoustical Society of America, 87
acoustic standards, 85
acquired deafness, 19–23
adventitious deafness. *See* acquired
  deafness
aging, 23
alerting devices, 62–63
American Athletic Association of
  the Deaf, 74
American Sign Language (ASL), 48,
  49–54, 52
American Speech-Language-
  Hearing Association, 22
antibiotics, 19
antioxidants, 80–83
Antonelli, Patrick, 38–39
athletics, 74
Atoh 1, 75–77
audiologists, 27–28, 30–31, 39–40
audiometry, 28
auditory canal, 11–12
auditory-verbal therapy (AVT),
  43–46

balance, 21
Battey, James, 81
Biderman, Beverly, 16–17, 24, 63
bilirubin, 19
Bird, Barbara, 70–71
BlackBerry devices, 62
bone oscillating test, 30
bones, of the ear, 12, 13, 14

camps, 73–74
Centers for Disease Control, 22, 41

Chandrasekhar, Sunjana, 78
childhood illnesses, 19
Clerc, Laurent, 48
closed captioning, 62
cochlea, 15, 75–80
  mechanical, 84–85
cochlear hair cells, 75–80
cochlear implants, 37–42
  attachment of external
    components for, 39–40
  potential problems with, 40, 41,
    42
  surgical procedure for, 38–39
  workings of, 37–38
communication aids
  auditory-visual therapy (AVT),
    43–46
  cued speech, 56–57
  sign language, 48, 49–54
  speechreading, 54–56
  speech therapy, 43–46
  Total Communication, 57–58
communication problems, 24–26
Conductive Hearing Loss, 11–14
congenital deafness, 16–17, 89–90
Cordero, Jose F., 64–65
Corrales, Eduardo C., 80
cued speech, 56–57
cytomegalovirus, 17–18

Dangers Decibels Project, 88
Deaf Awareness Week, 10
Deaf Community, 54, 74–75
Deaf Life (magazine), 16
deafness, 8, 11, 29, 43

assistive devices for, 60–63
causes of, 16–23
challenges of, 59–60, 63, 69–72
diagnosis of, 27–31
educational programs for people
  with, 63–69
heredity and, 16–17
misconceptions about, 6–7
physical effects of, 23–24
prenatal factors for, 17–18
prevention of, 84–90
research for future therapies for,
  75–83
treatment for, 31–38
types of, 11–17
Deaf World Games, 74
decibels, 23–24
Dogs for the Deaf, 70

eardrum, 12
ears
  balance and, 21
  components of, 11–15, 21
  examinations of, 30–31
  infections of, 19–20
ear trumpets, 29
ear wax, 11–12
education
  Gallaudet University, 64–65
  mainstreaming process, 65–67
  special programs, 63–65
  special schools, 67–69
*Encyclopedia of Deafness and Hearing
  Disorder, The* (Tarkington and
  Sussman), 13, 64
ENT: Ear, Nose, Throat Journal, 80
eustacian tube, 14

fetal alcohol syndrome, 18
finger spelling, 50–51
French Sign Language, 48
frequency modulation (FM) system,
  66–67
future therapies, 75–84

Gallaudet, Thomas Hopkins, 48

Gallaudet Research Institute, 19,
  64–65
Gallaudet University, 64–65
"Gene That Blocks Regrowth of
  Hearing Cells Identified for the
  First Time"(Web article), 81
gene therapy, 75–77, 81
genetics, 16–17
German measles. *See* rubella

hearing aids, 33–37
hearing dogs, 70–71
Hearing Dogs for Deaf People (Web
  site), 70–71
hearing loss
  communication difficulties caused
    by, 43
  prevention research, 82–83
  sensorineural, 15
  tests for, 27–31
  treatments for, 31–38
  see also deafness
Help for Hearing Loss (Web site),
  84–85
heredity, 16–17
Hertz, Heinrich, 19
hertz (Hz), 13, 24

inner ear, 11, 12, 13, 15, 75–80
Internet technology, 62

jaundice, 19

Kaye, Lori, 27
Kelley, Matthew W., 77
Kisor, Henry, 56

League for the Hard of Hearing, 84
l'Epée, Charles-Michel, 48
Levitan, Linda, 26
lipreading, 54–56

Madison, Ted, 22–23
Malone, O., Jr., 26
McCallum, Heather Whitestone,
  39–40

Ménière's disease, 21
middle ear, 11, 12, 13–14, 21, 30–31
Moore, Matthew S., 26
movies, 62
Mullins, Tina, 22

N-acetylcystine (NAC), 82–83
National Association of the Deaf,
    54, 74
National Captioning Institute, 62
National Center for Law and
    Deafness, 65
National Center on Birth Defects
    and Developmental Disabilities,
    64–65
National Foundation for the Deaf
    (NFD), 9–10
National Hearing Conservation
    Association, 22–23
National Information Center on
    Deafness, 65
National Institute on Deafness and
    Other Communication Disorders
    (NIDCD), 9, 77, 81, 88–89
National Institutes of Health, 20–21
noise, 20–23
    measurement, 23–24, 25
    pollution, 84–89
Noise Free America, 84
noise-induced hearing loss (NIHL),
    9–10, 20–23, 81, 84–89
Noise Off, 84
Noise Pollution Clearinghouse, 87
normal hearing, 23

oral language, 25–26
organizations, 74
    see also specific organizations
ossicles, 12–14
otoacoustic emissions test, 30
otosclerosis, 13–14, 31–33
otoscope, 30
outer ear, 11–12, 30
oval window (of the ear), 12

pagers, 62

prelingual deafness, 24–25
premature birth, 18–19
proteins, 77–78
pure-tone audiometry, 27

Quiet Classrooms, 86, 87–88

Rb1, 81
rubella, 17

school. *See* education
Schumacher, Marianne, 9–10
Self Help for the Hard of Hearing
    (SHHH), 73
semicircular canal, 21
Signed English, 53
sign language, 48
    characteristics of, 50–51
    finger spelling and, 50–51
    learning, 53–54
Society for Testing and Materials,
    85
sound conduction, 13–14
sound measurement, 13, 23–24,
    25
sound waves, 11–12, 13, 15
speech, 24–26
speechreading, 54–56
speech therapy, 46–47, 49
stapedectomy, 31–33
stapes, 13–14
stem cells, 78–80
Stop That Noise!, 88
summer camps, 73–74
support groups, 72–73
Sussman, Alan, 13

Tarkington, Carol, 13
telephone aids, 60–62
teletypewriter (TTY), 61–63
television, 62
tinnitus, 15, 21
Total Communication, 57–58
toxoplasmosis, 17–18
toys, 85–87
TRPA 1, 77–78

tympanic membrane, 12
tympanometer, 30
tympanoplasty, 31

vestibular system, 21
video relay service (VRS), 62
viruses, 17–18

vitamins, 80, 82

Watters, Karen, 80
What's That Pig Outdoors? (Kisor), 56
Wise Ears, 88–89
workplace noise, 22–23
World Federation of the Deaf, 10

Picture Credits

About the Author

Barbara Sheen is the author of numerous works of fiction and non-fiction for young people. She lives in New Mexico with her family. In her spare time, she likes to swim, walk, cook, read, and garden.